Caramel Tastes Like Candy

Written by

LAVIDA MORALE

ISBN: 978-1-4269-6410-7 (sc)
ISBN: 978-1-4269-6680-4 (e)

Trafford rev. 04/20/2011

 www.trafford.com

North America & international
toll-free: 1 888 232 4444 (USA & Canada)
phone: 250 383 6864 ♦ fax: 812 355 4082

Without inspiration life could be boring.... I would like to give thank yous to my friends and family for putting up with me. I would like to give a special Thank you to my biggest inspiration my son, Antonio Osorio for giving me unconditional love and the strength to want more in life; and to my special friend Shelley J. McWilliams for supporting me and giving me the courage to continue when writing a book was just a thought in my mind.

Intro Logue

What do you mean you don't love me after everything I have done for you, now you want to leave me and what's this shit I'm not what you're looking for in life I can't believe you're doing this to me. Carmella looked around for something to toss at Joshua. I can't believe your leaving me. Joshua said girl get yourself together you are a grown woman acting like a child having a tantrum. What do you expect you told me to stay in the house and do my womanly duties I did that shit because I love you and you asked me to. Now you want to leave me for what some corny bitch that sucked your dick. Joshua you told me you would take care of everything that had to do with the finances you know I'm not working and I haven't worked for over three years, now I'm going to be stuck with all the bills. Joshua looked at Carmella as her tears rolled down her cheeks and said well that's not my problem anymore you should learn how to save your money, now stop all that non sense with the tears you're a grown woman figure out a way to take care of yourself

Carmella lunged at Joshua to inflict some sort of pain on him with the knife she held in her hand, Joshua having the upper body strength grabbed Carmella by her arms and tossed her onto the couch in the living room. Just as Carmella was getting up the phone rang, when she answered it, it was Amelio he said hey Carmella its me I'm here to pick you up are you ready? Carmella came through the other line and said no I'm with Joshua and he just pushed me onto the couch. Amelio said WHAT! Without hesitation hung up the phone and within seconds Amelio was at Carmella's door banging on it to let him in. when Carmella opened the door Amelio went past her and straight to Joshua, not thinking straight he began to throw punches not knowing if they were hitting Joshua. The two men tussled back and forth for about five minutes before the broke apart from each other. Carmella did not know what to do she was holding her brother back as Joshua stood up from the floor where Amelio had left him. Joshua got up and wiped the blood from his lips, he said you gay ass mother fucker you just chipped my tooth. Amelio was yelling in Spanish, Carmella looked at Joshua and told him how he will pay for all the heart ache he has just caused her. She said Joshua I love you and wish nothing bad on you, everything you have done to me will come back to you; I hope you have a happy life with your new girl because she is going to juice you for everything you got and more. Joshua looked at Carmella and said you wish you had what I got but like I said your not the woman I was hoping to live my life with. When you get your shit together then you can call me, I will think about excepting you back into my life. Amelio looked at Joshua he said man if you don't get out of this house I'm coming after you again. Joshua grabbed his bags and left not wanting to deal with Amelio again.

Carmella sat on the couch to shed the tears for the man she was wanted to spend the rest of her life with as he walked out of the door leaving her with nothing but her clothes rent and a car note to pay. Amelio what am I going to do? I have nothing I'll be homeless. Amelio said don't worry I can help you out until you get on your feet, until then I don't want you around that guy I've told you before not to let that man control you. This is the exact reason men like Joshua are no good. All they like to screw people over to get what they want. Carmella shook her head and walked out of the house with Amelio promising herself not to look back at this time in her life when everything she thought she had was gone in a matter of minutes. How was that possible she did not know. Now her trust in men has become nothing but hatred.

Carmella had moved in with Amelio for a short period of time she has been working a regular Nine to Five job at minimum wage, she was tired and wanted a change. Carmella was getting ready to cook dinner for herself and Amelio when the phone rang. Carmella answered the phone she said hello…. Hey girl how are you doing? The voice on the other line belonged to Sophia one of her old neighbors when she was living in Fields Corner. Carmella said I'm good hanging in there, I was just about to cook dinner. How are you Sophia? I'm good, we all miss you down here I had to hunt your brother down to get a number for you. Carmella is everything alright. Carmella answered no I wish I had a better job so I can be on my own, having to depend on my brother for his help, it's bringing my pride down. Sophia said well honey I had to do a lot of sacrificing when Richard left us. Carmella said yeah you have a good job and you take very good care of your children. If I had children I would want to be a good mother like you. Sophia said if you knew the days and nights I cried because I didn't know what to do next or what was going to happen next especially with my children girl I had to get my shit together and fast for the sake of my children.

Carmella was still thinking about Joshua, she said I can't believe after so many years of being with Joshua that he would do me like that. Sophia said don't worry about Joshua he is living his life and not thinking about you now it's time you think about yourself. Carmella said I know I still have to find a better way of earning some money, working for a fast food joint is not paying the bills. Sophia hesitated then said well I can give you this number for the place where I started working, you can go into business for yourself and I just give you this one advice do not become partners with anyone. This way you keep all the money to yourself. Carmella didn't know what to say, she wondered what was Sophia talking about? Carmella said hold on let me get a pen and paper to write it on because I can't afford a cell phone.

After she was finished getting the stuff she went back to the house phone Carmella said okay I'm ready for the number Sophia. Sophia was on the other line giving Carmella all the information about the company and keeping out details on what Carmella had to do. Once Carmella got all the information about the company she said okay Sophia I'm going to let you go so I can call this number, I need something and fast. They both said their goodbyes and hung up the phone. Carmella picked the phone back up and immediately began to dial the number Sophia had given her. She listened to the automated system, Carmella went into a deep thought Sophia was such a good mother how could she do such things and then give me the number. Then Carmella thought about Joshua and what he has done to her. Carmella hit redial on the phone and started her own business….

Chapter One

My mouth was forced opened as he jammed his penis into my mouth forcing me to endure every bit of it. I tried to push away, his hands placed on the back of my head insinuating I wasn't going anywhere. My head bopped back and forth on his erection. Sucking on the pineapple condom hard, with every breath I took in. I knew he was ready to let loose, his face began to turn red. In one more bop of my head he released what he had inside of him. Oh yeah heck yeah he grunted. The tip of the condom was filled with semen. Yes I am a pro at what I do! Okay I thought to myself, now it's my turn to get pleasure from this Stinky man. I took the pineapple condom off his penis, and placed a regular condom on that mother. I pushed his nasty ass on the bed, and began to straddle his face with my vagina suffocating him like he had tried to suffocate me (revenge is a bitch) I thought to myself as I rode his face like I was riding bare back on a stallion. EAT ME EAME! I yelled oh yes that's how I like it the stinky man was getting his money's worth.

Once I felt my vagina pulsating I jumped off, I said I don't want to finish off this way I slid my hand back down to his penis and rubbed it back into an erection. Hmm yeah I'm glad I picked you Latin women are so hot to look at. Damn it they're as wonderful in bed too remind me to give you a tip when we're done here pretty lady. Ah I moaned responding to what the stinky man said I will as I maneuvered myself onto the erected penis, beginning in a slow rocking motion back and forth, up and down. The rocking got stronger, I felt his penis pulsating inside of me; I knew it was time to earn my tip. I lift up my leg and swung it over his upper torso, in a one-eighty degree turn without climbing off the his penis. At that moment I knew I had blown his mind, the Stinky Man grabbed my hips. With full force he thrust into my now swollen pussy. I couldn't help it I was enjoying the way he was doing me. Yelled YES do me, HARDER HARDER HARRRDERRR, were the last words I said through a convulsing body. A few seconds later I felt the stinky man give off an explosion. His nut was so intense it sent a chill up my spine. Damn I'm; I could pat myself on the back.

When we were done I got off the bed and wiped myself with the towel I had placed next to the bed. I got dressed, walked over to the stinky man putting my hand out. I said okay you're satisfied now it's time to pay. Wow you were amazing, what's your name again? Caramel like the candy! Enough of the small talk just pay me. Okay mamacita slow down I'm going to give you your money and a well deserved tip. The stinky man complimented me on my acrobatics. He said that thing you did when you twisted your body without getting off of my penis. Phew …. I need to teach my wife that one. I looked at the stinky man shaking my head dumb mother, why get married if you're going to pay me to satisfy you. Not my problem, I shook it out of my head. Telling myself, my rent and bills are paid for, I watched as he pulled a wad of hundred dollar bills out of his pant pocket. He slowly began to place them in my counting as he continued to check out my wholesome body. Not most women have my body figure, and the few that did didn't know how to use it to benefit their pockets. I was one of those girls until I opened my eyes to what was really out there and to be honest not much. I'm no model I think their too stinky, I do know that my body has men and women turning their heads to look and I loved the attention.

Anyways back to the stinky, he was counting really slow to keep me there a bit longer. I said hello are you going to pay? He said ONE… TWO… THREE… FOUR… I thought to myself come man EIGHT… NINE… TEN… he said there you go Caramel One thousand like you said. Oh and here' s an extra two the tip I had promised you. I hope to see you soon, I couldn't help but to respond to what he had just hoped for. As long as you have the money. He sat back on the bed Caramel he repeated my name. perfect name for a perfect woman, keep your line open I think I will be your number one client. I looked at the stinky man, sitting on the bed okay man enough talking I got to go wash up for the next man who thinks he's doing something. I said okay honey you know you're my favorite client, I might have to give this up if you keep spoiling me this. He said well caramel with a smile that will make the Statue of Liberty get up and run. You know my money will make you do anything I want. I looked at the disgusting man, he was absolutely right his money did make me do what he wanted, yet at the end of the day he was going home to his boring as wife thinking about the way I put it on him that's why he calls me. With a smile I responded to his comment…. I said well at this moment I did what you want, now it's time for me to leave. I walked out of the room, leaving the Stinky Man sitting on the bed of the Hotel. I left out of the hotel and flagged a cab down. When I got inside of the cab I told the driver where I was going. It only took fifteen minutes to get home. I paid the cab driver then walked into my apartment complex.

I live in Downtown Boston, with a view of the city. It's amazing just being able to look out your window and see what's out there. My mother had plans for me to be a hot shot lawyer I guess that was her dream, not mine. I wanted to become a great actress like the Nun from the movie where she sings and took care of the children… instead I'm doing what I am doing now and getting paid good money for it. Who can make a Thousand dollars in one hour, if the clients like it I get a hefty tip. My bank account is always on point. I walked into my apartment when my cell phone began to ring. Hello….. Um hi is this Caramel? I said yes it is whose calling? Hi it's Tim I mean Stan. Okay which one is it Tim or Stan? When I am working I never want to know your real name for a couple of reasons the first being it's personal information for just wanting to get some ass. The second one being if you have a wife or a girlfriend it's easy to say wrong number. The voice on the other line answered Stan it's Stan, we have a meeting tonight at Eight O'clock I'm just calling to remind you and to give you the directions to the hotel. I said of course as long as you have the money. He said in a nervous voice, yes of course I've never done this before so please take it easy on me. a lot of my clients like to role play. I go along with them. Caramel will take it nice and slow, don't worry your little head about that okay. He answered back in a shy tone of voice yes okay, then he continued to give me the directions to the hotel to meet him at, when he was done I repeated the directions to the Hotel then eight o'clock look professional. Okay Stan I'll be there and hung up the phone.

It was past Six Thirty which meant I had to take a shower, do my hair, get dressed, and grab a bite to eat. I always carry extra cash on me just in case of an emergency. I make sure that my clients are legit I don't want anyone to fuck with my money. Some of my clients were very picky so I satisfy them to the fullest, so they keep my bank account full. If I worked a regular Nine to Five I would not make not even half of what I make now. Of course I can't deposit it all into the bank account so I keep a safe in the apartment. I finished getting ready and left out of the apartment making my way down to the train station to make it to the Hotel in time. I wore my pin stripped suit on with a white Oxford shirt that showed enough cleavage, and my black pumps. I pushed my back into a bun and wore my most expensive reading glasses to make me look like a business woman instead of an escort. I got on the train and rode it all the way to the plaza, which was only a couple of blocks from the Hotel. As I walked down the street I could see how the men were turning to look as I walked past them, I was loving the attention.

When I walked into the lobby of the Hotel, it was six minutes past Eight O'clock. Stan was sitting at the bar looking irritated. I said hi sorry I'm late were you sitting here for a long time? He answered no not really, did you bring the stuff. Of course everything you like is in here. I patted the purse I was carrying. Stan nodded his head as he stood up from the stool he was sitting on. Stan lifted his hand insinuating ladies first, now the difference between Stan and the Stinky Man was Stan is truly a handsome man he has all the right facial features and his body is in incredible shape. Yet no one will ever imagine that he has a really really small penis. So whenever he called I would make sure my needs were met. Now I see why he paid for my services, because I made him feel like he was the shit. We got on the elevator and went up to the seventh floor. He had already paid for the room a day in advance; he used the key card to enter inside of the room. The room was beautiful with a nicely made bed, and a view of the Mass Pike. Stan had already told the concierge to bring Strawberries and Champagne so it will chill. Stan walked over to the Champagne popped the bottle open, and poured it into two glasses one for him and one for me.

I always want to make my clients feel comfortable before I get into work mode. I said Stan how was work today? Stan answered good I'm grateful it's Friday and I don't have to worry about it until Monday. Stan is a very successful accountant with Homafide Bank. I got the hint then changed the subject into something more sexual. Okay I said what can I help you with tonight? As I walked into the bathroom to change into something more exciting. Stan said well I have this dilemma, see I'm horny and you are the only one who can satisfy me right at this moment. I could hear him through the bathroom door, I said what's your dilemma you're horny? I walked out of the bathroom in my Lady Lingerie thong and matching bra it was fuchsia pink that complimented my complexion. Stan walked over to me and handed me a glass of Champagne. I took a sip from the glass, then I grabbed a strawberry and began to tease the fruit with my tongue before biting into it. I was giving this man what he was paying for, I took another sip of the champagne and walked over to Stan. I placed my left hand on his tiny penis to massage it, thinking how unfortunate this man is not to have been blessed with a good sized penis. I took another sip of the champagne and told myself okay Caramel it's time to get to work. I grabbed Stan by the hand after rubbing his penis and led Stan to the bed.

I said okay baby lets see what I can do for you tonight. I unzipped his pants to reveal the silky boxers. Hmm, I began to put on a front while I continued to rub his penis again this time through the boxers. I can't even give it a name like Jimmy or Mandingo it was more like a Wee Willie Winkie. I massaged Stan's penis to its full erection, which wasn't much. I grabbed his thigh bringing him closer to me. I thought to myself man I'm glad I got my shit off with the Stinky guy, I think if I hadn't done that I would've been a very upset escort right now. I said what would you like for me to do first? Stan looked at me I could see he was ready to let go of his frustrations. Stan said play with that vagina let me see the juices flow out of you. I laid back on the bed spread my legs in the eagle position, this way Stan could see every movement as I played with myself. I put my index finger into my mouth to get it wet then brought it down to my vagina, found my clitoris to stimulate myself. I slowly began to caress it, I said damn this shit feels good. The slow circular motions, up and down round and round. Aaah I can feel the sensation building up inside of me. My eyes rolled to the back of my head, OH STAN OH STAN! Stan stopped watching got down on his knees at the edge of the bed. He was low enough where I could feel the hairs of his goatee brushing up against my lips.

Stan gently blew on my vagina while I continued to finger myself. My strokes got stronger faster and harder, Stan moved my hand away hmm I could feel the wetness of his tongue as he slowly began to fondle my vagina lips, then my vaginas outer parts. SLURRRP I could hear him sucking up my juices like he was drinking a big gulp from the Quick in and out store. Hmm yeah that's it my body started to jerk as he swirled his tongue mimicking what I had did with my finger. My body began to jerk harder as I reached my climax. Aaah I grabbed Stan's head and stuffed it into my inner thighs I climaxed hard; Stan took it all into his mouth licking the lips of my vagina finishing the job. I lifted his head, still trying to catch my breath I asked are you ready for the next part? Yes Stan answered as he wiped his mouth of my juices. I walked over to the purse I had brought with me earlier to get the strap-on Stan had requested. Now it's not usual for a man to ask for a strap-on, but in Stan's case his penis is that small that he needs the Strap on to get his nut. I went to bend down to help Stan put on the Strap on. Stan walked over to me as I held the Strap On in my hand, I bent down to help Stan with the Strap On.... No Caramel! I got he said it so quickly I just backed off and let him put the gadget on himself.

After Stan put on the Strap On, he scooped me up and laid me on the bed. I kneeled on the bed as I caressed the plastic penis, kissing Stan's neck I told him how good it felt. Stan began to finger my vagina, when he felt it getting wet he said turn around Caramel I want to do you Doggie Style. I twisted myself on the bed I was on my hands and knees facing the opposite direction. I felt Stan's hand on the middle of my back and the other on my waist, as he pushed the rubber penis into my ass. Stan oh Stan, slow down your ah. At that point Stan grabbed my hair and pulled the shit out of it. I felt like he had pulled it from the roots. I said what the hell are you doing Stan? Stan said I'm coming, he was ramming the plastic penis into me hard. Shit work must have been real hectic for him today. Normally Stan is gentle with me. He began to yell YES YES UH UH. Stan released a lot of frustration with that nut; I thought to myself he just gave me a new ass hole with the way he was banging me. Stan said sorry I had a lot on my mind, I had to answer that I said shit I believe you as I got up from the bed in pain. When I looked at the time it was past Nine O'clock normally I want to high tail it out of the room, but I could see that Stan needed to talk. I switched the light back on, went into the bathroom cleaned myself and got dressed. I figured I would sit and listen to what Stan had to say without charging him for the remainder of the night. I walked back into the room, shocked at what I saw I couldn't help but to the way I did

I said what the heck is that shit? Stan was bending down picking up his pants when I saw the most disturbing shit. This mother fucker had two fucking parts. He had a penis and a vagina. I said oh my goodness, what the fuck is going on here? Stan gave me a surprised look, he said Caramel I could explain. I said yes please explain this shit to me. Stan began to tell me his life story, to make a long story short he was born with two genital parts the doctors call it a fancy name I call it a fucking hermaphrodite. Now I understood why his penis was so small, and why he got off wearing a Strap On he was confused. He had the body of a man a Wee Willie Winkie of a man and a vagina like me. Damn by the time I left the Hotel it was Eleven Thirty, I had to leave before I missed the last train back to

Downtown, Boston. Before I left out of the room I told Stan to call me if he wants to hook up again know well in the back of my head I was all screwed up from what I just saw.

While riding on the train back to my apartment I couldn't help but to think about Stan. This mother had two genital parts, and the one that gets the most pleasure is the vagina. Wow! I kept thinking to myself did I have sex with a man or a woman. My mind was going crazy to the point that the train attendant broke my train of thought with her announcement of the next stop doors and the doors will open on the right. That snapped me back into reality I'm ready to go home and just wash up and relax. Stan was in my head I didn't realize how far I had walked I was already in front of my apartment complex.

I walked into the building and was greeted by Jerry the security guard. He said Hello little miss how's it going? Now Jerry was old yet still had some strength to him. The first day I moved into the building two guys were going at it in the lobby. Jerry got on their asses, then warned them not to come back into the building causing anymore trouble, the next time they were going to have broken limbs. Jerry then went back to his regular demeanor. That scared the shit out of me, my mother always said the quietest ones are the toughest ones. After replying to Jerry I rode the elevator up to my floor and went into my apartment. Once I walked into my apartment. I turned off my telephones so I could get a good night sleep. I had to collect my thoughts on what just happened. I wasn't in the mood for friends, family, and clients. I thought to myself damn Stan messed my head all up, now I see why his shit was so small. Well from now on if a client has a dysfunction he would have to tell me that shit so I can be better prepared. I got into the shower, Lavender is the most relaxing smell to use, followed by some Chamomile Tea I didn't realize when I had fallen asleep.

Chapter Two

When I woke up it was Twelve O'clock in the afternoon, I was truly refreshed. Once I turned my phones back on they both began to ring. I answered my cell phone first I said Hello…. Hey girl what are you doing tonight? My gay as brothers voice echoed on the other line. He's longer than I am, and he's the daughter my mother always wanted me to be. Amelio became the hot shot lawyer even though he had to hide his sexuality throughout college. His sexuality helped him get a positions in one of Boston's top law firms. He made it and I'm very proud of him. Hey sis, what are you doing tonight? I said I don't know yet it's only Twelve in the afternoon. Why are asking? He said the reason I'm asking is because I want someone to come with me to this new club called the Diploma, and who better than my sister. I know that you will always have my back. I said okay Amelio what time are you leaving and two where is the club at? Amelio giggled on the other line, he said be ready by Nine Thirty and the club is in Rhode Island. I said okay I'll go, guess I have to go buy something nice to wear. I hung up the phone, and then got ready to go shopping. My phones were still ringing I ignored all the calls.

Nine Thirty came, I had gotten dressed with my Dark Blue jeans and beaded shirt, and my Stellos. I made my way down to lobby to wait for Amelio, I was talking to Jerry when a Platinum colored car pulled up to the front of the building. Thirty seconds later my cell phone rang…. I said hello little brother. Hey sis I'm outside I was excited he had told me he bought a new car I did not know it was a sports car. What is that you? I hung up the phone and ran out of the double doors. Amelio came out of the car, sometimes I can't stand my brother. He was dressed to impress, he wore his black expensive shoes, black slacks and a Platinum colored shirt that was the same color of the car. I asked when did you get this? He said yesterday and it rides smooth, now get in let's go party. Amelio snapped his finger and twitched his ass back to the driver side of the sports car without saying another word. The ride to the club was not what I expected Amelio had the music blasting, and for a lawyer he smoked a lot of Marijuana. We had a joint before we got to the club I was feeling relaxed. When we arrived at the club it was quarter to eleven there was no line so we got in quickly. The music was jamming, and everyone was on the dance floor. My wonderful brother kept one detail from me it was gay night. We walked over to the bar to get our drinks. As soon as we got to the bar the bartender asked what are you having? Over the loud music I said I want a cognac and cola. I turned to Amelio what are you having? Amelio said I want a Blow Job! I gave Amelia a funny looked then turned back to the bartender and said exactly what Amelio had requested. The bartender looked past me and right at Amelio, I could see they were into each other. I was amazed to see my brother in action something I have never seen him do that. I paid for the drinks and walked away. Amelio the bartender was checking you out.... I now Amelio said with a big ass smile. His name is Kevin he's the reason I'm here.

I said oh okay so I'm your decoy for you to get to know him. Yes and No Amelio answered, he's a law student he's doing an internship at my law firm. We got to talking and he told me what he does to pay for his tuition. I said cool but why a gay club. Amelio said Duh he's gay. Plus we give good tips if we like you. I said shut your mouth. The rest of the night Amelio and I drank, danced and made fun of people the whole nine. By the end of the night we were both shit faced. When the club was over we walked to the sports car and got in then called it a night. Well I called it a night Amelio had company the bartender actually went home with him, I thought to myself.... My brother got game. If my mother really knew what was going on with our lives she would disown us both. The good thing about that is she's in Puerto Rico and we are here in Boston so she won't have a clue of what's going on. Amelio dropped me off at home, I walked into the apartment, got into my bed and passed out. The next morning I woke up, my phone was vibrating, shit it felt good. I had fallen asleep with all my clothes on. I could feel the cell phone through my pants I was getting horny off of it. I'll ignore that one. I got off the bed and walked over to the bathroom, turned on the water to the bath tub and began to take off my clothes. Damn I was horny I needed to play with my vagina to make her feel better. I got inside of the tub my finger was doing wonders on my clitoris, I reached my climax within minutes. I put the shower on to clean myself better. When I got out I was feeling a whole lot better. I got out and dried myself off and got dressed then began my day I was debating whether I should take on clients or just relax at home.

My cell phone rang I looked at the phone my cliental had already began to call me the first call of the day was Jackson, now like said before I don't use real names for personal reasons, Jackson is the first client of the day. When Jackson calls I know that his wife is out if town. Hey Jackson, what can I help you with today? How did you know it was me? I thought about the question he just asked, then in a smart tone I said well we are in the Millenium and I believe it's the era of Caller ID. Jackson chuckled, his deep voice came through the line he said well it's been about two months; I want to tear that Beaver Dam up. I giggled and said well you know the price just tell me when and where, I'll meet you there. Jackson said I will have my driver go pick you up in an hour so be ready. I said okay I will be ready in one hour. One hour Caramel be ready then hung up the phone. I finished doing what I needed to get done as I was doing my stuff to get ready for Jackson I thought about how full of himself he really is. Like a lot of ball players I know, yet when it comes to getting down and dirty he really don't know what the hell he is doing half the time. I think he's on steriods, he climaxes so easily, his wife must be unsatisfied with him I know I am. I think that's why when he calls I make sure he is the first client of the day. He is what I call my quickie, the one to get my day started. It's funny how I get paid for a full hour and I'm only there for less than Thirty minutes including foreplay.

He's like a laughing Hyena, he smiles and makes the weirdest noises when we're doing the nasty. He does not have a paced rhythm it's more of a quick give it to me thrust and the sweat that pours out of this man is disgusting. Yuck! Oh my goodness let me go do what I have to so I can continue with my other clients. The black Town Limo pulled up to the building exactly one hour from when I had gotten off the phone with Jackson. Michael his Chauffer opened the door to let me in, once I climbed inside of the limo Michael closed the car door. He jumped into the driver's seat and took off. We were on our way to Brookline, where Jackson had bought a new studio apartment. When we arrived to the front of the three floor brick stone building, Michael got out of the car walked over to my door to open it. I couldn't keep my eyes off of him he was a beauty of his own. Michael stayed quiet as he let me out of the limo. I thought to myself if he had the money I would give him a taste of my vagina. I was curious I wanted to know what he had inside of his pants. Was it big or was it small, the mystery blew my mind. As I got out of the limo Jackson was waiting for me at the door of the brick stone building with a big smile on his face and the sweat already starting to form. Jackson said hello Caramel you're looking fine as always. I said thank you as I walked up the stairs. Jackson has many secluded locations this being one of them. No married man will disrespect his wife by bringing another woman into their home, that's her castle to reign over and if he did he really didn't love her to begin with.

I made it to the front of the wooden doors Jackson said after you. When I went inside of the apartment it was like I had entered a whole new dimension. It was scary, every where I looked I could see myself, all the walls were replaced with mirrors there was no color to the apartment the biggest thing there and the only thing that had color to it other than the furniture was a portrait of himself. I did not see one of his wife or his children just of Jackson. I looked at Jackson as he said how do you like it? I wanted to so you really are full of yourself but I kept it to myself and said don't you think it's a bit extreme to have so many mirrors on the walls like this? Jackson said nah, Caramel as he admired himself in one of the mirrors, one can never go to the extreme if you have the funds to do so. I rolled my eyes at his comment and walked over to the window from where I was standing I could see Michael was standing outside of the limo smoking a cigarette. I was looking at Michael and hadn't noticed when Jackson had came up behind me. I jumped when he placed his hands on my waist. He's a good looking guy isn't he? I was surprised at the question he had asked yet I gave him an honest answer. I said yes I think he is a good looking man. Do you want to have sex him? Again with the surprising questions, I said if he had the money yes I would have sex with him remember Jackson no one gets a free bee. Jackson continued to talk as he moved his hands from my waist up to my breast. You have succulent breast. Thank you I continued to look out of the window at Michael.

Jackson said his birthday is Monday in fact tomorrow, I will give you the money as a gift to Michael. I said okay call me about Michael tomorrow, right now my services belong to you. I turned to face Jackson, by his expression I knew he was more than ready to fuck me and release his nut. I took a step away from Jackson.... Grabbing his hand and leading him over to the couch. Having no time to pull out the condom from my back pocket, Jackson had stripped off his clothes completely. Oh goodness there goes that disgusting waterfall! I haven't started working this mother and his already letting go of all his bodily fluids. For a man with a good sized penis he really is corny. I took off my clothes and put the condom on Jackson, while he sat on the couch. I climbed on his penis and went right to work, I jumped on his penis really quick like he likes it. It was about five minutes later and Jackson climaxed. Oh Caramel oh oh Phew that was just number one, Jackson said as sweat poured out of his body. The apartment had good air conditioning I know for a fact it was just his body letting out so much sweat. I thought to myself does this man sweat like this when he is playing ball? This is a lot of sweat none of the other players would want to get next to him that's probably why he's become so famous no one will dear to interfer with the sweat man. I chuckled. Jackson said Caramel put it in your mouth, swallow it. I look at Jackson like he was crazy, he must be crazy if he thinks I'm going to out his penis in my mouth and swallowed anything that came out of him. I pulled out the pineapple flavored condom; it's my favorite taste and placed it on Jackson's penis. I started to work on my tongue on Jackson's dick swirling it around on the head of his penis. I could hear Jackson moaning; I took his penis and stuffed it into my mouth as far back as it will go. Once I felt my reflexes in the back of my throat, I pulled it out just enough to suck on it like a lollipop.

Jackson was more into it than I was, yeah that's it take it all into your mouth. Your lips are perfect, Hmm he began to wiggle his hips from side to side. I took the flavored condom off and placed a regular condom on him, he was not going to thrust my mouth with that quick motion of his. Knowing Jackson he would pride himself in knowing he was able to rip my lips apart while I gave him oral sex. Jackson jumped off the sofa swung me around, bent me over then rammed his shit into me. He was really anxious like he was in High School getting laid for the first time. Within four thrust of his dick Jackson gave out another nut. Wow I said like I was truly satisfied when I wasn't. what a rush! Jackson moved away panting out of breath, yeah that was a rush taking off the condom and placing it on the coffee table. We both got dressed, I looked at my watch it was exactly thirty minutes from the time I arrived to the Jackson was satisfied. We spoke for a bit about Michael and what services he wanted me to provide for Michael. I grabbed my belongings, Jackson walked me out of the apartment. Michael had noticed we both walked out of the apartment, he walked over to the car door to open it for me. Once I was inside of the limo and Michael had closed the door. I rolled down the window to hear Jackson tell me not to forget about tomorrow, he was going to call me to give me the time and place as to where to meet. I nodded my head then rolled the window back up. I told Michael to take me back home. I needed to get ready for my next client; Jackson is truly a waste of my time. Next time I'll bring some sort of potent enhancer to make him work longer.

I made it home just in time to shower and get ready for Dylan. I thanked Michael, is he really this quiet or is that a front. He let me out of the limo then nodded insinuating his good-bye. I couldn't help but to stare at him, he is truly a beautiful man, his skin the color of chocolate and his teeth are pearly white for a smoker, his eyes my goodness they are big and brown almost matching his complexion. I couldn't help but to admire his beauty. I walked away from the limo, I thought to myself yeah I'm going to give Michael extra services tomorrow. I walked into the building, I went straight to my apartment to get ready for Dylan we had spoken on the phone while I was inside of the limo. He was in town from New York City and wanted to get laid were his exact words. Dylan is a simple man all he wants is to get his shit off at every State he travels to without having to worry about commitment. It's understandable to me, I took a really quick shower to get all the sweat from Jackson off of me that is so disgusting. I got dressed then left to apartment to make m way down to The Restaurant Bar and Grille a nice bar and grille in the West End. Not too far from where I live. On a nice day like this I enjoy walking being able to see the scenery in Boston. The best part is the silly tourist; they come up and ask you to say certain words with the letter R in it like Park or Harvard. They get a kick out of hearing Bostonian not pronouncing the R. I met up with Dylan at The Restaurant he had already begun to drink at Four O'clock in the afternoon. Where it was too early for me I just ordered a Beer to refresh myself from the walking I had done to get there. I said so Dylan how is NYC? He looked at me; he was a very handsome man for his age. You would look at Dylan and not be able to tell he was over forty years old.

Dylan said it's quite well, I love it. Not to offend you Caramel he continued it's not as snobby as Boston. I said not all of Boston is snobby, just the places you have stayed at. Next time you come into Boston I will take you around so you can see that not all of Boston is not snobby at all. Instead the people will think that you are the snobby one. Dylan sat quietly, then responded okay maybe next time right now I'm looking at how fine you look in your casual clothing and I am liking it very much; those jeans fit you very well. Caramel I must say you are a fine specimen of our human species. I couldn't help it, I could feel my cheeks get red from blushing. I said okay um are you ready to get out of here? Dylan nodded his head he asked for his tab that he had opened. After paying at the bar we walked out of The Restaurant Bar and Grille.

Dylan and I walked to the Hotel where he was staying at, it was just down the street from the bar and grille. Dylan knew I enjoy the scenic views, so he got a room closest to the penthouse. When we walked into the room I was amazed at how elegant the room was, the view was amazing from the window I was looking out of, you could see the North End also known as "Little Italy". Dylan walked over to me and grabbed my hand to place on the bulge that was grew through his khaki's. I could feel his massive penis through the khaki's. I always ask my clients what they want done, but with Dylan he was simple whatever I did for him he would be satisfied. I unzipped his pants, they dropped down to the ground I pulled a Pina Colada flavored condom and put it where it belonged on Dylan's penis. I got down on my knees without moving away from the window. I opened my mouth as wide as I could open it and put Dylan's penis into it. Hmm I could taste the Pina Colada on the condom. My head bopped back and forth, he placed his hands on the top of my head gently stroking my hair. He was truly a simple man who liked it nice and slow at times. I kissed his penis until I got down to his scrotum and sucked on them, I moved back to sucking on his penis

Dylan stopped me; he said lets move over to the bed. I lay on the bed that was in the middle of the room with my head just off the edge of the bed. I said come here I grabbed his dick and stuffed it back into my mouth making gagging noises because it is so meaty. I could feel Dylan's inner thigh hitting my cheeks as he did small squats into my mouth. He went up and down, ooh I could hear the pleasure in his tone. Dylan stopped squatting; he leaned forward to unzip my jeans. I could feel his hand creeping into my panties; I continued to suck on his penis. Dylan moved away to take off my clothes, he said snatching off all my clothes without hesitation he was an experienced man with women. He went back to the squatting position when all my clothes were off. I went back to sucking on his dick, Dylan began to finger my clitoris the more I sucked on his penis the faster and harder he stroked his finger on my clitoris. I felt my body begin to climax, Dylan felt it too. He leaned down and began to suck on my clitoris, then blew on it and continued to suck on it. Ah it felt so good we did the Sixty-Nine position. I had to stop sucking on his penis, he was pleasing me to my fullest extent. Aaah I could feel an orgasm coming, to my body started to jerk uncontrollably. Dylan held my thighs apart as he swiveled his tongue throughout my vagina. I couldn't contain myself, I yelled out Dylan's name he continued to eat me out. I was amazed at this man.

Dylan had released the pressure on my thighs then rose back up to the squatting position. Now how am I going to top this shit off, he paid for my services yet he was the one pleasing me. I got up from the bed and laid Dylan on the floor of the room. I placed a pillow under his head to make him comfortable, I said okay now it's my turn to please you. I put one foot next to the top of his right shoulder and the left foot next to his left leg. I said are you ready? Dylan nodded his head, I did a complete split making sure that his penis was inside of me. I leaned forward to keep myself steady, and began to pump my ass up and down. I felt Dylan grab my ass I knew he was enjoying it. I continued to pump my ass, Dylan also started to thrust upwards into my vagina. Oh shit Dylan moaned as he let out his nut. I could see his eyes roll to the back of his head in satisfaction.

We both were done, I got off and laid on the floor next to Dylan. I said you have a nice tongue, I didn't know you had it in you. Dylan just looked at me quietly. It was only seven thirty, but after that workout it would be nice to get some sleep. Dylan finally spoke; he said what you thought I was a boring old man who likes to get pleased. I'm forty six years old with a lot of experience, I can teach you some things the tongue was just one of them. I said well today you have showed me and gave me more than I could handle. I got up to get dressed, Dylan stayed on the floor for a couple of more minutes then got up. He said well I have a conference meeting in the morning and need to get some sleep. After he finished I knew it was my cue to leave. I said I hope you enjoyed my services; you have my number call whenever you want I'll be available. He nodded his head then walked me to the door. I said until next time and walked out of the room. The elevator ride down to the lobby I made a mental note to use the split on other clients who might like it. When I left the Hotel the sun was setting. I tried to walk back home, instead I decided to take the train home from the North End to Downtown area since it was closer to my apartment. Dylan had worn me out and I needed to rest I didn't think that I would be able to take on another client after Dylan. I made it home got myself in relax mode thinking about ideas to please Michael tomorrow.

Chapter Three

When I got into my apartment after being with Dylan, my phone began to ring. I said hello... hey big sis it's Amelio are you busy? I said no I just got in the house I was about to relax, what's going on. I was beat but I could hear the desperation in his voice as he spoke. He said remember Kevin the bartender from the night club Diploma? I said yes you guys really hit it off. Amelio said yeah I thought so too. I have been calling him all day today and he's not answering his cell phone, he even sent me into voicemail a couple of times. I said Amelio what happened? He said well last night after I dropped you off we went back to my place, I had told him I would rather go over his place, but he gave me this lame excuse that it was out of the way. I should've known, well we went back to my place, got comfortable had some more drinks then got down and dirty. Today he woke up early and leaves without saying good bye, he just left me sleeping on the bed. Okay now I didn't care about that, I was able to sleep longer. Now listen to this Amelio told me. I'm calling him and he's not answering the fucking phone. I said to Amelio he's probably studying he is a law student. Amelio got annoyed that I had cut him off. Sis listen to the rest okay! I said okay finish telling me.

Amelio said the last time I called Kevin a woman answered his phone, his cell phone. Me being the dumb ass played it off like I was a co-worker she asked me if I wanted to leave a message and I told her no that I will try him again later. I said Amelio so he has a roommate. No Sis let me finish I could hear Amelio crying on the other line. I got nosy and I asked the woman who was I speaking to, and she fucking told me Nancy his wife. I was shocked to hear that… I said WHAT!   He didn't have on a ring when we were at the club or I don't remember him having one. Amelio said in a frustrated tone yeah that bastard didn't wear it at work either. He never mentioned it not once the whole time we spoke. I said Amelio what are you going to do now? Amelio said I'm going to give him hell, for playing with my emotions. Did he think that if he slept with me it would help him get one foot through the door, or I would hook him up with another law firm? He just fucked up big time. I said Amelio, okay relax breath; I explained to him that's how men are they go for what they want. Whatever is best for their needs use the shit out of the next person if not make them feel like shit and then they leave you. Why do you think I use men now after Joshua left I did what I needed to do and told myself never to another man get the best of me.

Amelio said yeah but why use me like that, just le me know what exactly you want from me I don't like surprises or the drama. You know what I mean Sis. I like people to be upfront with me. Tell me what you want in life and how you plan on getting there and if I could help you I would the best way possible, Amelio kept talking when he was done I told him the only advice I could tell him. I said Amelio when you go back to work, be professional I've seen you work your ass off to get to where you are now. Don't fuck it up because of a douche bag, just be corgel as possible and don't bring it up this way you don't have to deal with the drama at work. Amelio said you're right I'm not going to risk my profession over this asshole; I could find myself someone who actually cares about me. I'm just hurt, why couldn't he be honest with me. Kevin just proved to me that he is the type of person that would sleep his way to the top. He won't make it to far some one will bust his bubble. Amelio said well I feel a lot better since I talked with you, thanks Sis for listening to me. I said no problem even though I really didn't say much. We both giggled I told Amelio I have to let you go. I had this client that worked me today. Amelio I'll talk to later, I hung up the phone and prepared my well deserved shower.

When I got off the phone with Amelio I noticed I had a missed call from Jackson. I wasn't in the mood to speak to anyone other than my brother. I went into the bathroom and took my shower. When I out of the shower I poured myself a glass of White Zinfandel and ordered my favorite movie the one with the singing nun and the kids, main actress in the movie is incredible, she really is an inspiration to me. The cable company was playing that one movie all month long. I've must have fallen asleep early, when I woke up it was seven-thirty in the morning. I got dressed and went to Eat a Bagel for some breakfast. After I ate breakfast I began to clean the apartment, I got my laundry ready to take to the cleaners. My mind started to wonder when I was with Joshua I use to do all this shit, and he still stepped out on me. I won't ever let another man control me the way he did. When I finished cleaning I got in the shower got dressed and started my day. Once I was all dolled up, I picked up my phone to call Jackson back from last night. The phone went into voicemail; I was leaving Jackson a message when the other line began to ring. I looked at the caller Id it was Jackson calling me. I said hello I just left you a message to call me back. The voice on the other line was not Jackson's voice it was his wife's. she said who the fuck are you, and how do you know my husband. I said I'm sorry I thought I was calling Jackson, I tried to play it off but she had me. She said no bitch I saw your number he called you yesterday too, who the fuck are you? I didn't know what to else to say to the woman I didn't want to break up a family… okay Caramel think, think of something.

I said my name is Caramel I'm an escort. WHAT! The woman on the other line went crazy, I had to take her mind off the fact that her husband hired my services to please him. That's when Michael jumped into my mind, wow miss calm down I haven't slept with your husband, I had a missed call yesterday and a message that said he required my services for someone named Michael I guess it's his birthday today and that he wished to use my services as a gift to Michael. The woman on the other line was still talking I don't think she heard a word I said. I thought to myself I don't need this nonsense from anyone and hung up the phone. My phone began to ring again, this time I answered the phone with an attitude. The woman continued to insult me, now listen here you prostitute I thought to myself I should tell her about her husband and what it is exactly what I do for him. I ignored everything she had to say to me. Instead I cut her off in mid sentence, listen lady I got a call from your husband for someone named Michael his chauffer, where he got my number I don't know I don't advertise my services like that. All I know is that you need to stop calling me and harassing me, I could easily find out where you live.

The woman's voice was quiet and when I stopped talking she said bitch you don't know where I live and you won't find out either. The next time you call this cell phone I'm going to find out where you live and your not going to like it. I'm going to shove this phone down your throat since you like to put penises down your throat the phone should fit just fine. I was amazed at the threat she had made I had never heard that one before. I told the woman you don't have to worry about me calling your husband, just make sure to tell him if he still needs my services again to give me a call. I hung up the phone; this is why I don't give real names and if it wasn't for me flirting with the guy at the cell phone company my real name would have appeared on the caller ID instead of Caramel Delight. I was walking into the living room when my phone rang again; Jackson's number had popped up. I answered the phone and said listen lady I'm not sleeping with your husband he called me for my services, now stop calling me. When I was done Jackson came over the other line, he said hello… is this Caramel? I said yes it is! Playing along with Jackson, he continued by saying hi my name is Jackson please excuse my wife she got the wrong idea in her head. Yet I still need your services for my chauffer Michael. I said okay let me get a pen and paper to write down your instructions.

Jackson stayed quiet I could still hear his wife in the back ground talking shit. She said I don't think Michael needs a nasty bitch like her, what he needs is a good girl a hard working girl. A girl that's going to take good care of him. Not a five cent whore that's going to please him for two minutes then leave him. I could hear Jackson telling his wife to stay quiet and to mind her own business, it was his money he could spend it as he pleased. Jackson's wife stayed quiet as I came back to the other line even though I never went anywhere she didn't need to know that. I said hey Jackson I'm ready for the information, he gave me all the instructions on what he wanted me to do for Michael. He didn't have to worry about it I was excited to be able to have Michael, I had m own plans. I finished listening to what Jackson had to say, when he was done I hung up the phone. I looked at the clock on my living room wall it was almost Twelve in the afternoon. I ran into the bed room to look for my sexiest outfit to wear for Michael. Before I could get to the closet my cell phone began to ring. I looked at the Caller ID thinking it was Jackson's wife again. It wasn't.

I answered the phone, hello.... This is Caramel how can I help you? The voice on the other line came in quick and squeaky. The person said hi Caramel its Isaac and I'm ready for your services again. I went on tour last month, I couldn't find anyone to make me feel as worthless. Can you make me feel worthless today? I need to feel worthless it's the only way I can write better lyrics for my songs. I thought to myself *oh goodness Isaac the psycho path.* I said okay Isaac I have a very important client today, I can squeeze you in. I can come over right now is that okay with you. He said yes of course I can do that. You know my address I will be waiting for you Caramel. I told Isaac I would be there in a few minutes and hung up the phone. I wanted to get this over with, I had one thing on my mind and that was Michael. I left the apartment to catch the public bus to Isaac's house. I rode the bus about six blocks before it arrived close to Isaac's duplex. It was one thirty when I arrived in front of the duplex. I called Isaac on his cell phone, when he answered I told him I was outside.

Isaac is his real name, he is the only client that refuses to use an alias. I'm still not going to give him my real name... hell he'll probably stalk me. He looks like the type that will stalk a person and if he doesn't like what he sees, he'll kill you and the person you are with. That's why I always carry kid cut yah when I go to Isaac's. I have to have some sort of protection with me in case he tries something. I waited outside of the Duplex for two minutes before Isaac came to the door. I began to laugh as loud as I could when Isaac opened the door and I saw what he was wearing, even the couple that was just walking by did a double take and were giggling as the girl whispered something into her boyfriends ear. This mother had on patent leather shorts a choker and a muzzle in his mouth with no shirt on. When I walked up the stairs Isaac handed me a whip. I said okay I get, and then walked into the Duplex. I had to ask Isaac, what in the world are you wearing? I said Isaac I heard you've been a bad boy. Now I have to show you what happens for being a bad boy. I grabbed the choker, pulled on it leading Isaac into the living room. Isaac is single so I don't think he cared much for a relationship, he's a musician that likes his freedom. We walked over to the couch. I demanded Isaac sit down and don't get up until I tell you to. Isaac nodded his head, I giggled to myself he really looked silly wearing the muzzle. I had to take it out of his mouth. I would have laughed the entire time I was there. He watched as I undressed myself, showing off the natural bronze tan of my body.

Isaac reached up to touch me, I slapped his hand. I asked him did I give you permission to touch me. Answer me! Isaac shook his head no. now come here and eat this vagina. I lay on the rugged floor, and waited for Isaac got on his hands and knees stuck out his tongue like a thirsty dog. He began to lick my pubic hair, after the third stroke of his tongue he grabbed my left leg and lifted it up to the ceiling. He used his tongue playing with my clitoris, twirling it around and around, my mind lingered on the thought of me being with Michael will it feel like this or will it feel better than this. Isaac was one of my freakiest clients, what he lacked in motion he made up with his tongue. His tongue is abnormally long, he stroked that bad boy like he was licking a Frosty Ice Cream. With my leg being up in the air I could feel his tongue penetrate my vagina. In a low tone I whispered oh shit Isaac; he sucked on my clitoris to the point where it got numb. He went back to tongue fucking me; he continued to do it for about ten minutes before I climaxed, I lifted my head to see Isaac in those ridiculous shorts. I was still in Dominatrix mode I said now take off those shorts, and lay down on your back.

Isaac laid on the ground like I had told him to. I said your being a good boy, now I'm going to do something for you that's going to blow your mind. Are you ready Isaac nodded his head, answer me damn it! Yes I'm ready he had finally spoken. I knew that Isaac does Yoga so it wouldn't be hard for Isaac to do this. I squatted down and placed my hands on each side of his waist, I had Isaac push up as I squatted down. We started off slow, the movement got faster as caught onto what I was doing. His thrust became faster and harder, I felt like I was riding a mechanical bull. I yelled out Isaac's name, his eyes were rolling to the back of his head. I let go of his waist once he got into the rhythm, I stayed in the squatting position. I felt my legs beginning to shake I bent over to hold myself steady with Isaac's shoulder. I could feel the perspiration on Isaac's forehead. When I got closer to his ear I whispered into it Isaac this feels good…. Within a minute after that Isaac was groaning and squeezing my thighs. Wow Caramel that was wicked awesome he said through sweat and heavy breathing. I kept playing the role of a Dominatrix. I said now who told you to speak? Isaac looked at me then finished what he was saying. He said okay role play is over I thank you very much. I said that was fun, different yet fun.

Isaac said well I have to get ready for a gig, sorry to be so blunt. I said no problem I was here on business. I got up from the floor and put my clothes back on, when I looked at the guitar shaped clock over the fireplace it was almost Two- Thirty. Damn I am only good for one hour I must go. Before I could leave the Duplex Isaac said I have something for you. I said okay what is it? I was expecting him to come at me with a sharp blow to get me unconscious and stuff me somewhere, instead he handed me a bag from the Angel Long Department Store. I looked inside of the bag and found a pair of sneakers and a wristlet to go with the sneakers. I was thankful and shocked at the same time. I said how do you know my shoe size? Isaac answered with a smile don't worry I just do. That was spooky I grabbed my stuff including what Isaac had bought me and walked out of the Duplex. I needed to get ready for Michael so instead of riding the public bus back to my apartment I flagged a cab that was driving by. I needed to get home quick I want Michael to lose his mind when he sees me.

Chapter Four

When I walked into the my apartment cell phone began to ring, I answered it quickly as I moved towards the bathroom to take my shower and get ready for my date with Michael. Jackson had paid me Five Thousand to entertain Michael even though I would have done it for free, I was feeling Michael there was something about him that made me go crazy. Jackson's wife must be flipping out because he paid me so much to service Michael for one night. I said hello this is Caramel how can I help you? Amelio was on the other line raving in Spanish. I must admit we haven't spoken Spanish for a long time so it felt awkward to hear to hear him speaking it. I said Amelio slow down I can't understand what you're saying through all that yelling. Amelio took in a deep breath; he said Sis I've been calling you all afternoon, I'm about to lose my damn job! This fucking asshole, when I went into work today my Secretary Tina told me that one of the Partners was waiting for me inside of my office. I opened the door of my office and there he was sitting behind the desk on my chair. I stayed quiet as Amelio continued to vent about his problem. I said Good Morning, it took him a while before he responded. He just looked at me. I asked him if he wanted me on a case, usually when they're in your office that what they want, it's to tell you to be there second chair. Well that's not what he wanted.

He came into my office to tell me I was suspended without pay until an investigation is done on me. WHAT! I cut Amelio off investigation for what? Amelio said then Kevin went into work early this morning and told the partners that I was Sexually and Verbally harassing him. Then he told the Partners that I was calling his house causing stress on his wife and that the stress caused her to have a miscarriage. Sis all I could do was look at the man and ask him if he was joking with me. Amelio what are you going to do? I don't know I can't believe this shit is happening to me. I went into work today with the intentions of keeping it professional, but this asshole goes and does this sneaky shit. I got something for his ass, listen to this Amelio continued to talk, Dillon the guy that was sitting behind my desk told me Kevin had tried the same thing with him, he ignored his insinuations and kept moving. I should've done the same thing. Now look at my ass out of a job. About to lose everything and I wish I had something to prove that I was not the aggressor. I said well Amelio I was there that night when he was flirting with you, and I can tell your boss everything that happened that night, well not everything because I wasn't in the room with you guys when you were doing the nasty. I could try to help you anyway possible.

Amelio said thanks Sis, but I have to deal with this like a man I can't keep crying to you with every single one of my problems. I said don't worry about it you're my baby brother you're suppose to, I won't let nothing happen to you I promise. Amelio you are the only good thing I have in my life. Amelio said thanks, oh goodness I'm being gawked at by every fucking body that walks past my office door, I have to let you go. I said okay then hung up the phone. I ran into the bathroom took a shower I was pressed for time Michael would be here soon, my clothes were already laid out before I left the apartment earlier. I want to look my best for Michael, I really don't know what it is about him that drives me crazy every time I see him. He makes my pussy wet just thinking about him. I couldn't tell if it was the fact that he was so mysterious or that he was so handsome all I know is that I'm going to try to impress him tonight like he was my man. Damn Caramel what's going on in that head of yours? After what Joshua did to you, look at you falling for another one.

By the time I was finished getting dressed, it was quarter to Five and for some apparent reason my stomach had butterflies. Oh goodness I felt like a High School girl again. When the phone rang I jumped, it scared me I picked it up on the second ring. In a soft tone of voice I said Hello....it was Michael on the other line. Hello he said in a deep raspy voice, its Michael I was told to pick you up at Five O'clock. I was so excited to hear his voice that I stumbled over the umbrella holder. I have to move it from that area before I get hurt. I said I'll be right down, I rushed out of the apartment I didn't want him waiting for a long time. I got into the elevator, the Indian couple that lived next door also rode the elevator down with me. The couple looked at me them said hello to me especially the husband. I saw the his wife nudge him with her elbow. When we got to the first floor I let them out first from the elevator, I was rambling through my purse for my keys when I looked up Michael was standing in the middle of the lobby staring at me. I thought my heart had stopped for a minute. I said hello you look handsome trying to play it cool, like I wasn't feeling like I was about to lose feeling in my legs. Nice to see you out of your uniform. The black and white did you no justice at all.

Michael looked at me with a smile on his face, well that's what I have to wear for work. My boss told me about today this morning when I showed up for work, he gave me the night off. I walked closer to Michael, gave him a kiss on the cheek. Michael said I just want you to know I expect full service; just being able to talk will please me. I nodded my head insinuating I agree, my mind wondered as I looked Michael over. He is what you would call a real man. He had on a bluish gray button down shirt and black slacks. The whole outfit complemented his skin tone and beauty, he asked if I was ready to go I nodded my head again. What is going on with you Carmella? I thought to myself as he held the door open for me to walk out first. I looked at Jerry the security guard as I walked out, he motioned me to go with his hands. When we got outside of the building I noticed he was not driving the limo, he came in his own car which was the newest model black colored sedan. I was trying not to sound nervous even though I was. I said nice car, you must get paid well to be able to get this car. Michael looked at me as he opened my door first; he said yes I get paid very well by Mr. Jackson as you call him, when I got into the car he shut the door and walked over to the driver side of the sedan and got in. I thought this was probably a bad idea he was being so hesitant and his answers are so blunt.

I said before we drive off Happy Birthday, Jackson told me it was your birthday today. Michael said thank you as he drove off, I was trying to make conversation with the guy since he was being so blunt. I asked Michael did you get a lot of gifts, like he was a child. Michael answered me back no not really, I got some clothes from my and Mr. Jackson gave me you. I looked at Michael he was still facing the road, I looked away out of the wind. I said yeah he's not into me, I got into work mode which meant I wasn't going to take this opportunity to get to know him it was just going to be what I was paid for since he's not showing any interest in me. I said so what does Jackson have planned for us this evening? Michael said we are going to have dinner at Italian restaurant since I like Italian food, he also got me reservations to the Opera House…. And after that you are to do everything I tell you to do. I looked at Michael he had a big smile on his face, I felt myself get extremely wet when I saw him smiling. Man I want to fuck this guy putting my all into it. I don't belong to any one so I will tell you when the limit is got that….yeah I got it he said as he pressed play to turn in some music. When the music came on it was the song I hadn't heard in years. I looked at Michael and said are you seriously playing this? Michael said yeah why not the movie is great so is the music.

The next song on the CD was Mimi Love "Don't want to Fall in Love with You Again" I began to hum with the beat of the song. Michael looked at me quickly and said so you know this song? I said yes and I've seen the movie too! Michael nodded his head to agree, so what is your favorite movie? Michael asked through a grin. I said the one with the singing nun and kids, once I gave my answer to his question Michael began to laugh really hard. He turned his head to watch where he was going looked at me again and continued to laugh. I said what's so funny, I thought to myself all he needs to do is point his finger to let me know he is laughing at me. I was getting agitated with him for laughing so much at what I said. When Michael caught his breath after laughing so much, he said I have one question for you, do you do the turns when the nun is singing on the hill? I looked at Michael I snapped at him I said no I don't do the turns when the nun is singing on the hill I sit and watch the movie like a normal person. Michael said yeah okay you do the turns with the nun don't lie to me.

When we came up to a red light, Michael looked at me I told myself yes he does have a beautiful smile. He said Caramel I'm just joking with you, my little sister watches the same movie it's her favorite. When that one specific part of the movie comes on with the nun singing and turning on the hill, my little sister gets up and does the same thing. I looked at Michael I said whatever! You say your sister when you really mean your daughter. I was ready to pry Michael open like a can of Sardines. Michael said seriously my little sister watches the movie and does that shit. I asked how old is your little sister? Michael stayed quiet he went into a deep trance, I repeated the question I said Michael how old is your sister? Michael said twenty two. I said oh how cute she must really enjoy it, I rolled my eyes and looked out of the window. Michael said yeah she does, she has Down Syndrome, and the movie entertains her while my aunt does the chores around the house. I've been helping my aunt take care of her after my mom passed. I stayed quiet I didn't know what to say. I said I'm sorry; Michael looked at me then said why are you sorry, did you pass gas in my car? If you did make sure to hold your ass cheeks in that way the smell won't linger in my car.

I said I did not pass gas in your car, it's just sad to hear that about your sister. Michael looked at me he said don't be sad she is human just like the rest of us, even better she is the one woman that does not give me any shit. I turned my head towards Michael and I said I know how you feel, that's how I feel about my. He's the only one that does not give me shit about my profession. Michael said well remember I have one request from you he said be yourself tonight I don't need you to play it off only because my boss paid you. I turned to looked at Michael again; goodness that smile of his is a killer. Be myself….. Michael said yes be yourself. I'm being myself. Michael said you said that was a front you put on for people when they pay for your services. Well I didn't pay for your services so I would prefer that you act as you would normally act when your not around clients. I said well my services were paid for today so you are my client. Michael said okay so your going to pretend like you like me. I said no that's not pretend it's real I do like you. I realized what I had said and stayed quiet. Michael had a grin on his face, oh so you do like me or should I say you want to bang me. I started to blush, he noticed…. Fuck he noticed me blushing.

Michael continued to tease me; he said am I making you nervous your red there. Do I need to open the windows so you could cool off since I'm making you hot? I looked at Michael, I responded to his nonsense. It's my job to please you how ever you like tonight. That's what I was paid for and that's what I'm going to do, no you don't make me hot this weather makes me hot. Michael looked at me; he noticed that he was getting under my skin, in a good way. I said and another thing I don't live too far from the North End, why is it taking fifteen minutes to get there? When I looked at the time on the dash board it was exactly five thirty. We pulled up to the got out of the car, Michael went to pay the meter while I walked inside of the Italian restaurant. The host walked over to me and asked if I had reservations just as I was about to answer Michael walked into the restaurant. The host ignored me, as he recognized Michael, he said Michael good to see you again, not working today I see. Michael smiled and said no I'm not working today, the host looked around as if he was waiting for someone to walk in through the door then he said with a deep Italian accent; Michael where is your sister and aunt. Michael said no not tonight.

The host lifted his finger at Michael insinuating that he would be with him once he was done with me. The host said sorry miss do you have reservations tonight? Michael came up behind me and put his hand on the middle of my back, he said we have reservations it will be under my name. the host looked at Michael then back at me, like he was surprised to see us together. The host said Michael she is a beautiful woman, would you like the usual table by the window. I looked at Michael I quietly asked him do you come here a lot? Michael said my sister likes this place, so every month I bring my aunt and my sister to get them out of the house and out of the hood for at least one day of the month. We live in Dorchester, and getting away is good once in a while. I was so excited I said I lived in Dorchester two years ago where do you live? As we walked to the table Michael said if I tell you where I live you promise not to stalk me. I couldn't help but to giggle, I said yes I promise not to stalk you. Michael said I live in Saving Hill. Oh okay I nodded my head not too far from where I use to live, I was closer to Fields Corner.

When we got to the table Michael pulled out the chair for me then seated himself. The waiter came by he asked if we wanted anything to drink after placing two glasses in front of us. I looked at the fancy glasses. The setting was very elegant; Michael was looking at me, it was like a stare that spooked me out. He said can I ask you a question? I was being a smart ass I said your already did. Michael said ha ha nice one no I want to ask you why do you do this line of work? You're a beautiful sexy woman, yet you exploit yourself to these jerks? Do you not value yourself? I was shocked at the question as I thought shit he got me with these fucking questions. I told Michael I don't exploit myself, I'm doing something that I like to do and that is act like another person as long as I know who I am. I do value myself very much if not I would not make the amount of money that I make now. I can't see myself working a Nine to Five on a daily basis flipping burgers, in this profession I pick the days and hours I want to work and I don't have to deal with the bullshit. I get to pick who I want to deal with and if it works I keep them on my client list if it doesn't work out I won't deal with that person anymore and I would let them know why.

This profession pays my bills, rent and very expensive shopping habits. Michael said I see you're simple yet expensive at the same time, how is that possible. I said it's simple I'm a home body I really don't go out unless its with my brother, and when I go to the stores I want the most expensive thing I could find because I know I can get it. When I was a little girl I wasn't able to get everything I wanted. My mother was a single parent cleaning toilets for a living paying her way through school and taking care of both me and my brother. So I tell myself whatever I couldn't get when I was a kid I spoil myself now. Not only that if I decide to have any children I want them to have everything I don't want them to suffer like we did even though we were a happy family we were poor. My mother paid her way through college and once she got her degree she started working for Public Schools, and stayed there until she retired a few years ago. My father left her when I was about two years old. Came back a couple of years later, got her pregnant with my brother then left again. So basically she struggled the entire time she was raising us. I told myself I don't want that life for me. At one point she wanted me to become a lawyer, I've always wanted to become an actress. Now my brother is the big shot lawyer.

Michael looked as I continued to talk about my family, oh my goodness I haven't spoken like this to someone in a very long time…. It felt good. Michael cut in when he thought he could get in a few words before I began yammering again. He said your mother did all this, where were you guys when she was working? I said we stayed with the neighbors and sometimes we were able to go with her to work, until me and my brother were old enough to go to school. Michael said so basically your father played your mother like a fool gave her two children to raise on her own and became a dead beat father. I said yeah yet my mother worked hard to keep both of her children happy. She put my brother through college, and I talk to her once in a while. She still is upset because I didn't become a lawyer or a doctor. I decided to take my chances in acting, that didn't work so now I'm doing this. Since I came from I want to have as much as I can. This way again whenever I decide to have children they don't have to struggle like I did growing up. Michael stayed quiet then said I guess I was born with a y sliver spoon in my mouth compared to your life story. I had both my parents.

My father worked for the Sewer Company and my mother worked as a secretary for an insurance company. I'm the oldest of three children I have my sister and a brother the youngest one of all three. He fucked up his life he is now serving time, man he screwed up his life. I could see the hurt in Michael's eyes as he spoke about his brother. Is that the reason he is always so quiet. Michael said he's serving time and he's not twenty one yet. My mother passed away four months ago from Cancer. I said what about your father. He passed a few years back from a heart attack. I said tell me more about your sister…. Michael said well she was born with Down Syndrome the doctors say it is hereditary, my sister is as bright and beautiful than any girl I know…. I was being a smart ass I said including me? Michael didn't know how to answer the question. I said I'm just joking see I have some humor inside of me. So Michael how is she? Michael looked at me and said who? I said your sister…. She has the mentality of a child and the body of a woman, so I have to keep all the sick bastards that try to take advantage of her away. I kept asking question after question not noticing that Michael had ordered for the both of us until the food was brought out to the table. I asked where did it come from? Michael looked at me like I had just asked a really stupid question.

I had to rephrase the question, I said which one of your parents had the gene since you said it was hereditary. I didn't go to college, I do watch a lot of Reality TV…. Michael chuckled at what I had just said. Michael said my mother was French Canadian and my father was African, Michael continued to break it down to me while we ate. He said when I did the research it said that the Sixteenth Chromosome is a gene that a lot of the French Canadian people carry in their genes without knowing they have it unless they get tested for it. Where it comes from I really don't know because I'm not a doctor as you can see. I know that my mother was one of the few that carried the gene. I said and what about you? Michael looked at me he said no I don't have my mother tested us after my sister was born making it her priority that we knew what can happen using my sister as an example. I said well that was good so if you have any children you know what to him/her tested for. After taking the last scoop of pasta and placing it in my mouth, I asked Michael do you plan on having children? Michael said yes at one point in time I thought I was ready for children, now that I look at it I'm not ready and I have to find the right person who is willing to deal with everything I dish out. We finished eating had a couple glasses of wine and headed to the Opera House to go see the show

When we arrived at the Opera House it was close to seven thirty and the show was about to begin before we walked in Michael turned to me and said I really enjoyed your company I haven't been out in a while with work and helping my family. I want to thank you in case I forget at the end of the night. I looked at Michael and smiled, I said no problem we might be able to do this again another time other than tonight. Michael smiled at me; I would like that very much. We walked to our seat to watch the spectacular performance. I was amazed at all the costumes the dancing and the singing. I could feel Michael looking at me. The show had ended and everyone was standing applauding the performance I stood along with them wanting to yell out BRAVO like the other people. Once we walked out of the Opera House Michael said well I guess our date is over, I'll take you home if you want. I looked at the time on my cell phone it was only quarter to ten. I asked Michael would like to end the date or continue you have me for the rest of the night. Michael said what is there to do on a Monday night? I said there is plenty to do I didn't want Michael to see that I wanted him to stay around longer. I said we can walk around the Common's it's beautiful at this time of night with the lights, or we could go bowling and your last choice is you can come over to my apartment and have a couple of drinks and talk some more. Michael said having a couple of drinks at your apartment sounds good let's do that. I said okay we can do that I have plenty of liquor at the apartment; we both smiled at each other then got into the car. I said to my apartment we shall go….

When we arrived at my building complex, Michael looked a bit nervous I said are you okay? don't worry I wont bite you like a vampire…. Michael looked at me smiled then opened the door to let me into the building. Jerry was sitting in the same spot I had left him when I went on my date earlier in the evening with Michael. Jerry nodded his head and continued to look at his magazine. Michael and I walked to the elevator; I pressed the button to call for the elevator, Michael stopped me half way into the elevator he looked at me then asked do you have any pets? I said no I have non don't like furry little things running around in my house I think they are to messy for me. I said why you don't like them? Michael said I like animals I just can't be around them I am allergic to there fur. I wouldn't want to ruin the rest of our date by sneezing and coughing all over the place. I said no I have no furry creatures running around in my apartment, you're safe.... The elevator ride up to my level was quiet Michael had his hands stuffed in his pockets like he really was afraid of me. We arrived to the level where my apartment was on. I said to Michael this is where were getting off.... Michael followed me off the elevator and to my apartment he watched as I stumbled to find the keys inside of my purse. Michael had made a comment that my purse was not organized and how he noticed that I was doing the same thing when we had first met up with me in the lobby. I finally found the keys when we got to the front of the apartment.

I unlocked the door I told Michael with a grin on my face other than my brother you will be the second man that has entered my apartment.... Are you ready? Michael said yes I'm ready and honored to hear that. I opened the door and flipped the light switch to turn on the lights. Michael looked amazed like he was a kid inside of a candy store. Michael said you have a lovely home, I said thank you its my place of Zen. I don't bring my clients here they might go psycho on me, know what I mean. Michael said you have me here now your contradicting yourself..... I jumped back at Michael I said how am I contradicting myself when you asked me not to treat you like a client did you forget about that comment you made earlier. Michael stood at my door with a smile on his face, I thought to myself this guy really likes to smile. Throughout the whole date he has either had a smile or a grin on his face. I can only think of two reasons first one he enjoyed the date and the second is that smile is permanent like one of the rappers I always here about. Michael finally broke into my thoughts by saying you're right I was wrong now how about those drinks? I told Michael to have a seat on the couch while I made the drinks I asked what would you like? I have an assortment of darks, lights, and wine.

I turned to walk over to the mini bar when I felt Michael come up behind me and twirl me around. We stood face to chest his tall masculine chest was close enough for me to smell the cologne he was wearing the expensive shit for men it was an amazing tasty smell. Without any hesitation Michael kissed me with his lips touching my in a deep passionate kiss. I felt like he was a crack head feigning for his dope. Michael then released the pressure of his lips making the kiss feel more of a tender I want to fuck you right now kiss. His lips were juicy soft and very soothing I did not want to stop kissing Michael. I tried to push away thinking he will then apologize for what he just did. Instead Michael had a strong grip on me. With my eyes closed I could feel Michael ripping off every bit of my clothing, I didn't want to stop him then, he had gotten my vagina wet. When I decided it was time to open my eyes Michael had stripped me down leaving me with my under garments on. I said Michael you have to stop, why Michael answered as he continued by taking off my bra exposing my dark brown nipples. I thought to myself no time to waste this is the only time I will get to enjoy this man and I want it to be a great experience for him as well as myself…..

I stood naked in front of Michael with only my thong, I felt Michael moving his hands from my breast down to my waist and finally to my thong to remove those too. He got on his knees as I pulled my head back, my mind began to wonder this man has gotten me naked in front of the door oh shit the door I looked back to make sure that I had closed it when I walked into the apartment. It was closed! Michael stood there I could see the bulge growing inside of his pants. He undid his pant bottom, I could hear him unzip his pants as I unbuttoned his shirt, Michael kissed on my neck gently as he moved his finger down to my clitoris he wiggled his finger back and forth taking the same finger and poking it deep into my vagina. I took my foot off the umbrella stand, then got on my knees and began to kiss Michaels' inner thighs up to his scrotum going back down to his inner thighs. Michael let out a loud moan almost as loud as mine… I pulled down the black slacks Michael was wearing to expose the erected penis it was big and meaty, Michael was a well endowed man I stared I thought this shit is bigger than nine inches, I still wanted this man even if it meant getting a hysterectomy when he was done with me. I kissed the tip of his penis before I opened my mouth wide to endure not even half of it. I bopped my head back and forth a couple of times when I felt Michael stop me. He bent down and picked me up off my knees, lifting my leg up once again and placing it on the umbrella stand.

Michael shocked me when I felt his wet tongue then his lips sucking on my clitoris, I loved the feeling of it. Taking my leg off the umbrella stand and putting it over his shoulder to bring me closer to his face. He sucked in all the juices that came out of my vagina. I was wet, it felt like Niagara Falls at one point. When I reached my climax Michael continued my body jerking uncontrollably I couldn't feel when Michael had stopped licking on my vagina he was up and close to my ear. Michael whispered into my ear with his deep raspy voice where is the bed? I grabbed Michael's hand and lead him into the bedroom before we were inside of the room Michael had swooped me off my feet and carried me to the bed. Once he laid me on the bed Michael said close your eyes….. I didn't know what it was about this man I trusted his every word. I did as he said, I felt Michael's tongue work it's way from my leg up to my vagina making me jerk a bit more then up to my lips. Another passionate kiss that melted like Cotton Candy on my lips.

Michael said in a low tone Umm Caramel you taste like candy, right then I felt Michael penetrate my vagina with his Mandigula dick! I gave out a loud grunt then held my breath as he slowly thrust his penis into my vagina. Once he was in his rhythm I let out the breath I was holding in. I enjoyed it the way he stroked his body I tried my hardest to keep up with Michael I also tried my best not to climax. Michael was hitting the right spots I could feel the passion something I haven't felt in a very long time. I couldn't contain myself anymore I yelled out Michael's name as his thrust became faster telling me he was ready to let out his nut. When we both reached that point of climax I said Michael   I'M   COMING I'MCOMING OH MY MICHAEL I'M COMING HARD! I yelled as everything I had inside of me exploded out, my eyes closed tight as I wanted to control myself and yet I couldn't. when I opened my eyes I could see that Michael had the same experience I had he made a face I can't explain. The bodily fluids we let out were all over the bed, after that eruption I could still feel Michael's body jerking as I squeezed my vagina lips making him jerk simultaneously.

Michael rolled next to me afterwards, he said I could use that drink right now if you don't mind. We both laughed I said yeah I think that is a good idea I need a drink also…. I was getting up from the bed when Michael stopped me half way and said no don't get the drinks just lay here with me. I laid back down next to Michael I felt him put his arms around me to hold me. I let my body relax I never been held like this not even from Joshua it felt good I liked it. For the first time in two years I did not need a lavender shower or the Chamomile Tea to put me to sleep this man has done it in just one try. He was Michael Burria the boxer that night he did a TKO on me. I closed my eyes and don't remember falling asleep.

Chapter Five

The next morning when I woke I felt all over the bed, Michael was gone like a typical man. They will wine you dine you fuck you then leave you, without even saying good-bye. Yet I was angry and hungry.... I was upset Michael had left without saying good-bye I thought we had a good night and the sex was passionate. I told myself I was paid for services last night it wasn't a real date so I brushed it off my shoulders he was another client even though it bothered me I was hungry I wasn't going to dwell on him, yes I am. I got off the bed I wanted something to eat.... My mind wondered here I go with the same routine as always. When I looked at the time it was Eight Thirty, I walked into the bathroom which was right inside of the room I thought it was convenient being inside of the room because I didn't have to walk half way around the world to brush my teeth. I grabbed some pajamas from the dresser as I walked to the dresser my vagina was sore I said damn Michael is that big I could still feel the pain from last night.

After putting on the pajamas I walked to the bathroom and closed the door. I grabbed my tooth brush and tooth paste I was mad how could Michael leave I feel used usually I'm the one leaving without any feelings. I was brushing my teeth in deep thought when I heard a knock at the bathroom door. Who the fuck is knocking on my door I was scared shitless, this mother fucker left my door open and some stranger is inside of my house. I scrambled to look for something sharp to defend myself with, I found the scissors that I keep inside of the medicine cabinet. The knock came again this time I could hear the deep raspy voice come through the door... Hey I see you woke up, my heart skipped a beat. It was Michael he didn't leave he was still here. I brushed my teeth as quick as I could threw the brush back where it belonged then opened the door. When I opened the door I was amazed to see Michael with no shirt on showing his masculinity. All Michael had on was his black slacks and socks, I do like the form of Michael's demeanor it was exotic and tantalizing

When I walked back into the bedroom I felt like an idiot with the teddy bear pajamas I had on. Michael grinned then comment on what I was wearing.... You know there is nothing more sexier than those teddy bear pajamas I did know they still made those things. I said well they do and you better not hate on them they are very comfortable. Michael said no not at all. I asked what are you still doing here? Michael said I have the day off and my aunt and sister are in Virginia visiting family, so I decided to surprise you to say thank you for last night it was amazing. I said you think so, I could have done better. I looked at Michael as he spoke to me in a charming manner, so early in the morning and he still has swagger. Michael interrupted my thoughts when he said well I know you have things to do so I will get going I made breakfast incase you were hungry I hope you don't mind. I said I would like something to eat I am starving.... Hi starving I'm hungry nice to meet you. Michael had said through another grin. Michael I called his name in a tone that was playful I said please don't say that corny ass line ever again it does not suit you not one bit... Michael's grin turned into a laughter as he said well Caramel I cut him off please call me Carmella that is my real name. okay Carmella breakfast is in the kitchen enjoy. I wanted him to stay a bit longer I just opened my mouth and let out what I wanted. Am I going to be eating alone or will you like to join me. Michael said well it's up to you on what you want me to do I'm free the whole day. Michael said plus I don't want to get in the way of what ever business you have to handle today.

I said you don't have to leave neither of my phones are ringing, it's Tuesday no one calls me on Tuesday' unless it's my brother or my mother calling me. I said Michael your not getting in my way, now let's go see what you made for breakfast. You know I am an expert food critic, if I don't like how it taste you would have to leave and if I like it you just might be the one. I giggled as I flirted with Michael batting my eyes. Michael gave out another laugh, he said Oh I can cook that's one of my many thing's I can definitely do right. I said amongst other things, I grinned at Michael as I walked past him in my teddy bear pajamas not worrying about taking them off. We both walked into the kitchen and to my surprise he cooked for a family of eight instead of two people. Michael saw my facial expression before jumping in, I didn't know what you liked or wanted to eat so I made what I could. Michael had cooked Eggs, Bacon, Sausage links, and Pancakes I couldn't help it I asked what you thought you was cooking for a cow? Michael looked at me before responding then said I looked in the refrigerator and took out what ever I thought you might like and cooked it now have a sit. I sat on one of the stool in the kitchen as Michael served me a plat with everything he had made then he served himself a plate of food and sat down besides me. We both sat and ate our food quietly Michael waiting for me to criticize the wonderful breakfast he worked on making me.

I said wow Michael this is some grade A shit, where did you learn how to cook like this? Michael said being the oldest child I spent a lot of time helping my mother with my sister and brother. I would also go to school smelling like Bacon sometimes it was funny the other kids would hate it, they said every time I came around them I made them hungry again. I laughed at what Michael just said. I asked Michael through a mouth full of pancakes, Michael your mother never told you to enjoy your childhood? Michael put his head down then responded he said no she needed my help with my sister and my father being at work, she didn't have anyone else to help her and my Aunt was living in Virginia at that time. When my father had his Heart Attack that's when I realized I had to step up as the man of the house I was about fourteen years old. My mother made sure that I went to school and got an education, watching my mother deal with a lot I couldn't enjoy my childhood I couldn't see her suffering like that. Michael was telling me his life story as we ate breakfast, all I could do was sit there and listen to everything he said to me. Michael continued he was telling me about his brother when he had gotten in trouble how his mother was devastated.

She couldn't take anymore of the luck she was having, one day she felt really sick I could hear Michael choke up as he was telling his story… one day my mother felt sick and went to get herself checked, the clinic had ran some tested on her a few weeks later she was diagnosed with Ovarian Cancer. Michael kept talking and I continued to listen. Michael said I guess she was tired of living the Cancer ate her up quickly all the money from my father's life insurance and the money they had saved up went on paying the house, medical bills and the medicine my mother needed as well as my little sister's needs. We barely had money left over to get a lawyer for my brother. I was working at Foot Lockers when my mother past I was in debt and struggling. While I was working at Foot Lockers a co-worker brought in this magazine the ones that are out on the streets and you can just grab one. I was looking at the magazine and saw this one Ad the company was looking for drivers willing to work seven days a week. I looked at Michael without saying a word I said to myself he is really opening up to me, does he feel comfortable around me. While Michael continued to talked I thought well he did make breakfast for me, I wonder if he was interested in me the whole time and didn't say anything I snapped myself out of my thought and finished listening to Michael tell me his life story up to this point.

Michael said when I called the agency it was a Temp thing if the contractor liked me then they will keep me if not they will utilize me until my services weren't needed anymore and I would move on to the next client that needed me. There was only one position left and the guy said if I wanted it I could for it. Michael said the next day I brought in my resume, my drivers license and all the other information they had asked me for. The man at the temp agency gave me the name and the address where I needed to show up when I saw the name on the pick up card I thought I had lost my mind for a minute. Michael looked at me I was like a child listening to a bed time story. Michael asked if he was boring me I said no not at all I am intrigued. The way you're telling you're story is like it changed your life. Michael said well it did I was excited he was one of my idols.

Michael continued to talk about how it was to work for Jackson, he said it was cool the first couple of months, I was able to see the different places, he would take me along with him to different cities as his personal assistant it was a nice gig. To be honest Michael looked at me the whole time he was on the away games he was very faithful to his wife. After about two months Jackson had decided to hire me permanently, Michael shook his head. Michael continued as I stayed quiet, once I was hired permanently by Jackson it was like hell had broke loose and ended up inside of that house. That family is dysfunctional, I have never seen anything like it that is a screwed up couple. Still they remain together, Jackson's wife is Satan reincarnated she is the worse one of all. I think the only sane one in that house is the kid. Jackson and his wife are off their bonkers with the shit they do to each other. I was intrigued by what Michael was telling me about Jackson and his wife, we had finished eating and moved over to the living room where it was comfortable to sit. Michael said Jackson's wife is a snobby spoiled bitch that thinks she can get everything she wants without having to work for it. She only married Jackson for his money she says it all the time to him. She is a sneaky, evil, deceitful woman I don't blame Jackson for doing what he does behind her back now. Michael continued to talk I had no choice I listened as Michael told the weird and crazy shit that goes on in Jackson's home. Michael got my full attention when Michael began to tell me about the time Jackson's wife threw herself over him. I said no way Michael gave me a grin then said yeah really.

It was one time only when Jackson was on an away game I couldn't go I had to help my aunt with my sister so he told me to stay and accommodate his wife…. She had paged me one morning telling me that she wanted to go shopping and that she didn't feel like driving to go and pick her up. Michael said when I arrived at the house she looked as if she was ready to go shopping it was the fall so she wore a light Trench coat. I opened up the door to the limo when Jackson's wife said she had forgotten her purse the night stand of the master bedroom, she said would you please get it for me I will wait right here. Michael gave me a smirk; he knew he had my attention. He said I told her I would get her purse and would be right back, I went inside of the house to get the purse I had ran into the Nanny and asked her where was the master bedroom. When I found the room I went inside of it have you ever seen the show with all the houses of famous people and how they made it up? Well there's was one of the best one's on the show. It's a basic black and white color with a zebra print rug but the layout of the room is amazing it could be made into a one bedroom apartment if they ever needed the money.... Well when I grabbed the purse and turned to walk out of the room guess who was at the door waiting for me? I said Jackson's wife..... Michael nodded his head yup! She walked into the room and closed the door behind her she undid her trench coat and revealed a very sexy lingerie she was wearing, her body is very built like she goes to the gym every day and she wears her hair short which suits her. I still wasn't attracted to her I like Jackson I think he is the coolest boss I've had in years and the schedule wasn't that bad. Anyways she got closer to me and told me that she wanted to fuck my brains out of my skull those were her exact words... I laughed cutting Michael from finishing, of course you being a man gave her what she asked for.

Michael shook his head he said nah he wasn't my type and at that time I was in a relationship. Jackson's wife is the type that goes for what she wants and if she doesn't get it she will fuck you over in a heart beat, even if it means ruining someone's life. I explained to Jackson's wife that I was engaged to someone, she didn't care she was very adamant about getting inside of my pants. The bitch even offered me money like I was a man whore. I looked at Michael and said don't forget who your talking to. Michael apologized he said I didn't mean to offend you. She was crazy all ya'll women are crazy when you don't get what you want. Was got close enough to me then pushed me onto the bed and jumped on me. Michael said she is strong I had to wrestle the bitch off of me Jackson's wife was not taking no for an answer. The Nanny must have heard the commotion when she was walking by that she opened the door to the bedroom and startled both of us. I was actually relived that she had did that, Jackson's wife climbed off of me and went towards the door she pushed the Nanny out into the hallway then slammed the door in her face. That had given me enough time to get up off the bed. I walked over to the door and when she turned around she had this psychotic look on her face like she was going to kill me. I told her right then and there I quit…. Then stormed out of the room, I walked all the way to the bus stop mad as hell I liked the job I just couldn't deal with her. The Nanny got fired on the spot for walking into the bedroom the way that she did. I said yet your still working for Jackson. Michael said only because the Nanny called Jackson on his cell phone and left him a message to call back it was urgent. When Jackson called she had told him everything his wife was doing behind his back I wasn't the only one she was after….

She did the Cleaners if they were her type, the Gardeners and I think the Nanny said she was with a few of the other Chauffers before getting fired. That woman told him everything, as soon as Jackson got back into town he called me up and told me everything then offered my job back with a few exceptions. I would only work for him what ever happens we keep it between him and I his wife will have no control over my duties and the only time I would drive his wife around would be if the kid was in the car too… I said that's why she was so upset when Jackson was on the phone with me she still wants you and can't have you. If she does she will lose whatever Jackson has in the bank for her. I changed the subject on Michael I said so what happened to you being engaged? Michael said we weren't happy together she wanted the family thing and I wanted to be financially ready before bringing kids into this world so we broke everything off she went her way and I went mine, I haven't dated since. I said you have had your share of women though….

Michael said no you're the first woman I have been with in about a year. I said bull shit you went without for a whole year? Michael said yeah I mean I had my hand to give my penis a work out once in a while but I held off on having sex. I asked Michael so what made you change that last night? Michael said those pants you had on yesterday fitted you nicely I got closer and kissed Michael on the lips when I was getting into the passionate kiss my house phone began to ring, I said who could it be at this time in the morning. I said of course it's my brother and his men problems. Michael looked confused he said you mean woman. I said no I said it right men my brother is Homosexual, Michael was choked up he didn't know what else to say. I said don't worry he won't come onto you that's my job! I gave out a giggle and went to answer the phone. I answered it before the last ring.

I said hello Amelio what's going on I have company, I can't really talk right now. Amelio said well sis that company is in for a rude awakening because I'm downstairs in the lobby, I have some papers I need you to sign. I have to get all this shit done and over with before the investigation is finished. If I could prove that Kevin came onto to me first I swear on everything I have that I am going to destroy that man's career. I said okay Amelio come up stairs bring me the papers then you have to go okay. Amelio said it's not Joshua is it? I'm coming up right now... I said no Amelio it's not Joshua just bring the papers so I can sign them okay then hung up the phone. I walked over to Michael hey um you might be meeting my brother sooner than I thought he is on his way up here to bring me some papers. Michael still had his shirt off. He got up and ran into the bedroom to get his shirt to put it on. Michael walked out of the room with his shirt on the buttons weren't on the right way, Michael said I needed to put this on I don't want your brother drooling all over me and shit like you do. I looked at Michael. I said whatever, you're the one that went after me remember I was calm cool and collectives. You were Mr. Octopus with your hands all over me, putting your hands where ever they could reach.

Michael was about to respond when there was a knock on the door. Amelio was at the door, it only took him a few seconds to get to my apartment. Hey Sis open the door I have people out here staring at me like I'm a freak, as I walked over to open the door Michael ran I into the room to put on the shirt he had on the night before. I opened the door to the apartment Amelio did not wait for me to invite him in he walked in Amelio began to act like a drama queen okay where is he I know its not Joshua up in here after everything that Negro put you through. Amelio yelled out Joshua's name come on out you vagina, Amelio was walking towards the bedroom door when Michael came out with a grin on his face. Amelio said hi your not Joshua….. Michael shook his head no I'm Michael, Michael had his hand out as he introduced himself to my dramatic brother. Michael strode next to me to stand at my side. Amelio said wow big sis you must really like this guy if you let him stay the night in your apartment. I could feel myself blushing…. Amelio where are the papers you want me to sign. Oh there right here in my tote. I looked at Amelio you mean your man bag, he said you call it what you want to I like it. Amelio changed his attention back to Michael, so how did you meet my sister. Michael said she was a gift from my boss, and a wonderful gift. Amelio grunted then said so you were another client of hers. Carmi you know better than to bring your work home with you. Michael could see that I was getting frustrated with the comments Amelio was making. Michael jumped in on my defense, she wasn't working last night Carmella was my date. I hope you could respect that…..

Amelio looked at Michael then back at me honey if you paid for it you call it whatever you want. Michael came back he said I didn't pay for it it was free. I could feel the tension between them I said Amelio how about some breakfast? There is food in the oven go serve yourself a plate while I sign these papers. Amelio asked what did you make? I didn't cook Michael cooked while I slept wasn't the nice. Amelio said yeah whatever that is nice and romantic. Michael bent down close to my ear to whisper into it… I think I should go I don't think he likes me and he keeps rolling his eyes at me. I told don't worry about my brother he's harmless. He'll leave in a minute.

Michael said okay then walked into the living room while I began to sign the papers Amelio had given me. Amelio followed behind Michael while he munched on the food he had served himself. With a mouth full of food Amelio asked Michael so what do you do for a living. Michael said I'm a chauffer, wow Amelio said so you drive people around all day don't you get tired of that? Michael looked at Amelio and figured he could deal with his obnoxious ass a bit longer. No I drive one family around all day and I get breaks in between so I won't get tired it also gives me time to do what I need to get done.

Amelio said and that's come here fuck my sister and leave. Before Michael could say anything else I jumped in Amelio's face waving the papers he needed me to sign. Amelio if your having a rough time with your life it doesn't give you the right to treat my company like shit. What the hell is wrong with you? Amelio said I don't want to see you hurt again big sis I want to know where is he going in dating you, what work he does and shit that is all.

Michael was fed up with Amelio he said I work and take care of my family and I do like your sister unlike you I think you are a prick but what lawyer isn't. Amelio looked at me and asked are listening to this shit. I said yeah I'm listening to both of you and I want you to stop. Amelio did not like what I was saying he snatched the papers out of my hand then walking towards the door he made sure he let me know. I will call you and let you know when you have to go testify, next time answer your phone. Amelio walked out of the apartment slamming the door behind him. Michael came closer to me he put his arms around me wow your brother is a piece of work where did all the attitude and questions come from? Amelio is just protecting me I told you about Joshua he does not want to see it happen again, not only that he is going through a lot right now with this case filed against him.

I said enough about my brother he is gone lets go take a shower, Michael said I don't have any clothes I should really get going. I said don't worry about that I would run to the laundry room and put the clothes to was until then you can walk around in my robe. Michael looked at me then said I would love to take that shower with you. Point me in the right direction and I will follow you. We both went into the bathroom to take our shower. I ran the shower with hot water to let the steam run, both Michael and I took off the clothes and got inside of the shower. Michael looked at the body wash I had inside of the soap holder that was hanging from the shower head. You hae no manly soap in here. Why should I you are the only man that has been inside of this apartment... actually you are the only man that had as been inside this apartment since I have moved here. Michael responded I am honored. In grabbed the body wash, squirted it onto the sponge. I began to lather Michaels well built physique. Wow in the two years that I've lived alone. I haven't felt the experience of being with someone I really want to be with and here is Michael in my shower spending the day with me. I was excited…. Michael had turned to face the opposite direction as I washed his back, then turning to face me again. I could see that he was getting turned on b the way I washed him up. Michael's s penis was hard…. I had to make fun of Michael I said one touch from me and you get like a rock. Michael said yeah to top it off when I saw you in the sweats I couldn't wait for your brother to leave. I said yeah I couldn't wait for him to leave either he was brining in me down with his misery. Michael grabbed me bringing me closer to him; Michael started kissing on my neck. He told me to close my eyes and to raise my arms in the air.

I did everything Michael had told me to do without any complaints. I could feel Michael as he moved up and down my body me with the wash cloth gently stroking in that one area that made me weak. My pussy was throbbing wanting Michael again for the second time. I could feel Michael's over sized penis poking me in stomach. I thought to myself he is no Stan with his girlish ass and he definitely is not the stinky man, Michael is exactly what I had expected him to be…… A MANDINGO WARRIOR! I felt Michael thrust his penis into my beaver dam without any warning. He lifted me up grabbing my thighs and wrapping them around his waist. I thought we would slip since we were in the shower. My arms quickly gripped his bulky shoulders to keep myself from slipping. I looked into Michaels eyes and noticed the passion in them, I couldn't believe I'm letting this man have sex with me without a condom…. Are you crazy the thoughts ran crazy in my mind. Yet I didn't care he was what I wanted and I got it right in front of me.

I began to yell out Michaels name with every thrust he gave, it felt like a blunt object was being stuffed into my vagina. I enjoyed every bit of it. Michael stopped his thrust quickly spinning me around was now facing the shower wall; he pulled me back just a little space to bend me over. Once I was bent over he jammed his penis into me again. I could feel his hands on my shoulders as he quickened his thrust. My hands were on the shower wall trying to stop myself from banging my head. Michaels thrust got faster and faster, he was hitting my G- spot and I was liking it very much. I started to whine my body to his rhythm, within minutes we both gave out a big explosion of bodily fluids. When it was done and over with we both began to laugh and giggle. I said I hope you know this is the second time we have done it without a condom. Michael looked me in the eyes… maybe next time we would have to use them. I couldn't help it all I could do is roll my eyes at him then smile at the comment. The water was beginning to get cold we washed up fast and got out of the shower. Michael didn't have any clothes on him so I gave him one of my robes while I ran to the laundry to put his clothes to wash and dry. When I got back to the apartment Michael was sitting in the living room with the robe on and his leg crossed one over the other one like a woman. Michael said if I were to be in this when your brother was here earlier he would've raped my ass….

I looked at Michael and said you better leave my brother alone, he is my only friend, and I don't think he like the fact that I had you in my apartment. Michael asked why is that? I looked away then looked back at Michael I said well about two years ago I was dating Joshua the relationship I had told you about last night, we were living together, well Joshua had convinced me to stay at home and he would take care of all the finances, all I had to do was take care of the house. When Joshua got tired of me he used the lame excuse that I wasn't what he was looking for in life and left me stranded with nothing in our account to live on, I had to sell my car and do other things just to survive. Before Joshua left, he and Amelio got into big fight. Amelio knocked a couple of teeth out…. Michael stopped me he said wait a minute Amelio did what? I nodded my head, my brother may be fruity but he will defend his family to the fullest. He also got in trouble with his firm because of his conduct. From that day on if I liked someone he would have to be approved by my brother.

Michael looked at me with a raised eyebrow, he said so he better like me after he ate the food I made for you. I laughed even though it wasn't that funny, I felt happy for the first time in two years. I grabbed the remote from the coffee table and turned on the television, to our surprise the first thing that popped on the television was the movie of the singing nun …. Michael turned to look at me; hell no we cannot watch this movie I've had enough of the twirling Nun…. I said alright I won't put you through that torture. I flipped through the channel until we found something we agreed to watch, I don't know what go into me as soon as I laid my head on Michael's shoulder I fell right to sleep. I had the confidence of when I woke up Michael would still be there. I opened my eyes to the noise of the after traffic honking their horns. I stood up to stretch the crick out of my neck. I could see his face shining as he slept. I walked over to the kitchen and opened the refrigerator to see what was in it. I was hungry and I knew when Michael woke up he would be hungry too….

I looked at the clock on the stove, it was quarter past twelve. I felt like the day was going by fast. I felt relaxed in my apartment to the point where my day was almost gone and I was happy not doing something or doing someone. Michael had kept me in the house that day and it felt good. I pulled out the chicken from the freezer to out it to defrost, when I looked back at Michael I had noticed he was still in my robe, I placed the frozen chicken in the sink and ran to the laundry room where I had left Michael's clothes washing. When I opened the door to the laundry room and walked inside I found Michael's clothes on top of the laundry shelf with a note I capital letters the said "HOPE YOU DON'T MIND TOOK THE LIBERTY OF DRYING THE CLOTHES NEEDED THE WASHER APT 111". I was shocked that someone would do that, I grabbed the clothes and went back to my apartment.

When went inside my apartment I placed his clothes on the bar, I heard a voice ask your making chicken? I jumped not imaging that Michael would be up. I said yes I wanted to make you something for dinner…. Are those my clothes on the bar? I grabbed the clothes and handed them to Michael then said I should kidnap them that way you won't have to leave and I could keep you here as my personal slave, until someone decide to come looking for you. Michael looked at me slowly grabbing his clothes out of my hands, he said if you ever kidnap me my aunt and little sister will find me in a heart beat. They're half hound if you know what I mean. Michael raised his eyebrow and said they will find me where ever I am. I giggled at the joke, well I got off the subject I will begin to cook this dinner Mr. Chef please feel free to help with making your own dish. Michael said as soon as I get my clothes on and get out of this feminine robe I will help you as a matter of fact don't touch anything I will show you how it's done. Michael disappeared into the bedroom to put on his clothes, when he walked back into the kitchen he shooed me away and said I will call you when the food is done.

I think I could manage this by myself, I said okay if you think so I asked Michael would you like a drink? Some wine or something more power to it. Michael looked at me then answered in a girly voice, I will take the wine if you don't mind. I said I don't mind at all you just better start cooking that food. We both laughed as I walked over to the mini bar to pour out the wine. I sat and watched as Michael cooked the Chicken Alfredo, when he finished cooking we sat and at, then talked fir a bit before Michael said it was time for him to go…. It been really fun chilling like this but I have to work tomorrow and its getting late my aunt is probably worried about me. I will give you a call when I get home if that's okay with you. I said sure I'll wait for your call and I really enjoyed myself thank you. We both stood up and walked towards the door; Michael leaned over and kissed me on the lips that made my knees buckle. I opened the door, said good night I will see you soon. Michael agreed then walked out of the apartment, I watched as he made his way down the hall and into the elevator. Will Michael be my sweet heart, I thought to myself as I walked back into my apartment closing the door behind me. Everything was running through my head so quickly, I walked into the bedroom threw myself on the bed falling asleep with a huge smile on my face, yes Michael was exactly what I expected…..

Chapter Six

The next couple of weeks I was in La-La land, I didn't take on any clients especially Jackson. My days and nights were dedicated to talking on the phone with Michael. Even Amelio was the last of my worries, though he was going through a tough time was happy for the first time in a while. I really didn't want to hear about the drama that happened with Kevin. I felt like Amelio's misery was going to bring me down, it was the last thing I want right now. Michael and I have been talking on the phone for hours the past few weeks with Michael. We have so much in common, yet we are two different people. I was getting ready to go to the gym when my phone rang.... It was Michael, in an angry voice talking gibberish because Jackson was giving him shit at work about how he got us together, how I fucked him that I was nothing but a whore. At one point, he said I was going to take all of Michael's money then leave him. I was shocked to hear what Michael was telling me, only because I didn't think Jackson would go so low. I said well honey I'm an escort not a whore remember that, I have my own money I don't need yours, so the next time Jackson gives you shit just smile and say well at least I can please her and she doesn't have to fake it......

Michael began to laugh so did I, Michael asked did you really fake it with Jackson? I said Michael you would pick me up, within half hour I was done... you tell me if I faked it or not. Michael said well I hope you didn't fake it with, I said no baby you got the real deal. If you want I could show you again tonight. Michael said I wish I could I have to pick up the witch tonight then take her to the Casino, I won't be back until late. Michael said how about tomorrow? I said I can't I have a client and he paid for the whole night. Michael said well can I come along? No you can't come along it would feel weird brining you along for the ride. Yeah your right Michael agreed that it was not a good idea. I think we can go out for dinner on Sunday. Michael said fine that like a plan. We made the plans then hung up the phone; I walked out of the apartment when the phone rang again. A man with a deep accent was on the other line. Hello is this Caramel? I said yes who is calling? The man said it is Dajuan, calling to see if I can set up a day for me and my brother.... We would like to see you again before we go back to Africa. I went into a deep thought aww my African twins with their over sized penises. Man the last time I was with them I had to stay in bed for a couple of days, I was only able to take a shower and that alone was painful. Hello you still there Dajuan was still on the line. I said yes I am here how can I help you again after coming back into reality. Dajuan repeated himself asking if my services were available for them today we each have the money to pay such a beautiful woman for her services.

I was excited I said sure, right now I am going to the gym and after that I am free. Dajuan said in his heavy accent okay I will text you all the instructions on where to meet us once we make the reservations, I said okay just don't make them too late. Dajuan said we won't oh and Caramel please bring your favorite gadgets... I said sure thing honey, then I hung up the phone. I kept the phone on vibrate and placed my headphones in my ears, started listening to my favorite music. I walked out of the apartment, and down the hall to the elevator. I pressed the button to call for the elevator, it was taking a long time to come down to my floor. When it finally arrived I got in to find the same Indian couple getting on with me. The woman said something in their language the man looked at me and put his head down. I pressed the button to take us to the first floor; Jerry was at his usual spot reading a magazine. We all got out of the elevator. I waved to jerry as I walked out of the building. I was in my apartment for so long I had forgotten how hot it gets in Boston during the month of August.

I put on my sunglasses and started walking down Tremont St. until I got to the corner of Tremont and State St. where the gym was located. I walked inside of gym, after processing my ID I walked straight into the locker room. I changed into my gym clothes as I finished changing I noticed a skinny Blonde on the other side of me with her shirt off. It was obvious she was showing off her boob job. I walked past her to get a better look at her boobs, I was ready to work out all the fat that I had gained over the past few weeks I have been hanging with Michael. I started off with the treadmill for about thirty minutes, then made my way to the elliptical machine for another thirty minutes. When I was done doing my cardio I had decided to push myself a bit further so I took a class in aerobics for about forty-five minutes. All the straining from the class was starting to catch up with me. I was feeling tired yet good at the same time, it was a weird feeling. When I was done I didn't think of changing out of my sweaty clothes I was going to get my shit out of the locker room and go home.

Once the aerobics class was done I walked out of the room, straight to the locker room to grab my things. As soon as I walked in the same blonde was there again showing off her breasts. I got closer, I said they did a good job on your chest, the Blonde looked at me then said thank you my boyfriend paid for them….. I love showing them off! I said well good for you, then kept walking to my locker to grab my stuff. The Blonde finished getting dressed and was leaving at the same time I was walking out of the door. Just outside of the I thought I had seen a ghost, standing in front of me was Joshua looking miserable. All the memories of the last time we were in the same room came flooding back into my head.

I was shocked to see Joshua I hadn't noticed when the Blonde had walked past me and into Joshua's arms. The Blonde kissed Joshua on then said honey she likes my boobs…. I came back to reality when I felt the phone vibrating in my pocket, I pulled it out trying not to sound nervous. It was Michael on the other line I was happy, I said hey honey what's up. Michael had asked where was

I…. I'm still at the gym let me call you as soon as I get out of here okay. He agreed then hung up the phone. I looked back at Joshua and the Blonde she was down tying her sneakers when I walked up to them both I said hey Joshua long time no see how is everything? Joshua had his hands in his pockets trying to avoid eye contact with me, everything is good could be better…. And how are you? I'm fine just peachy, got my own things, own business going everything is working just fine for me I only needed someone to push me into that reality of not depending on others for my needs. Before Joshua could say another word the Blonde jumped in wow you two know each other, this is a small town. Joshua asked no kids yet? No I don't want to make the same mistake I made before.

I need to know who I am dealing with before I decide to have any children. Joshua looked away then back at me, yeah I know what you mean. The Blonde jumped in again, yeah Joshua wants children I don't I don't want to ruin this body, so we both agreed not to have any children. I said wow that's a nice agreement a life time together with no children, and how long have you two been together? The Blonde said about two going on three years. I said really well you two have a happy lifetime together. The Blonde said thank you that is so sweet…. I want this bitch to know who exactly I was, oh how rude of me since Joshua didn't introduce us what's your name? the Blonde said your right he didn't my name is Samantha, everyone calls me Sammy. I said well my name is Carmella it's nice to meet you.

Once the Blonde heard my name she stood back a bit like she was on defense, or like I was going to attack her ass. I should have yet I know I was the better person in this situation. I said it was nice to meet you; she looked at me and in a low tone said it was nice to meet you too. I couldn't help but to give a grin the bitch knew exactly who I was and yet didn't know me. I walked away from the both of them, with my last words being have a good night. I wasn't expecting it the Blonde said hey would you like a ride home? I said no thank you I live on Tremont St. my condo isn't too far I can walk…. I looked at Joshua who still had his head down then walked out of the gym without saying another word. Once I was out of the gym I took a deep breath then exhaled, I didn't know I would react so calm when I ran into Joshua…. I bet he is kicking himself in the ass right now for letting me go.

It was close to Seven Thirty when I got out of the gym, I called Michael back as soon as I walked out of the gym…. I couldn't wait to tell him everything that happened. I walked and talked to Michael over the phone as I made my way home. When I got to the front of my complex I told Michael I had to let him go, I needed to get ready for a client. We said our good nights and hung up the phone. I quickly went into the building needing to get ready for my African twins, I needed to get ready fast I ran past Jerry instead of waiting for the elevator I went up the stairs seven flights I was exhausted yet I needed to get ready. I got to my apartment once I was inside I headed straight to my closet to get the simplest thing I could wear. I found my favorite toys and stuffed them inside of my purse, I jumped into the shower after getting everything ready to take the smell of sweat and musk off of my body.

After taking a shower and getting dressed I heard my phone ringing, I knew I had left it on the bed but for some reason I couldn't find it. When I moved my covers I was able to catch the call on the last ring. I said hello whose calling? Amelio said well I see how much you love me Sis, you don't even call to see how I am doing. Thanks a lot… I said stop being a Drama Queen Amelio, I am not being a Drama Queen I expect you to be there for me like I was for you when you needed me that's all. Besides Amelio kept whining I'm about to lose everything my job especially all that I have worked so hard for gone….. The one man I thought I wanted to spend the rest of my life with is married to a woman and is claiming that I ruined his marriage and his wife. What do you want me to think Carmella?

I said don't worry little brother; everything will turn out for the best. Has anyone from the office called you or told you anything about the investigation. Amelio said no not yet I tell you this much I wish they would hurry up. I said so Amelio you haven't spoken to anyone in the office that can give you some sort of information about what's going on. Amelio stayed quiet for a few seconds before he answered. He said I spoke to almost everyone in that office if the investigators find out I did that I would get in more trouble than I already am in. Not only that everyone has told me the same thing they did the interview answered all their questions and when it was over nothing else was said to them again about it. I could hear Amelio whining through the phone I hope I get my job back Sis, I feel like I have lost complete control of my life and don't know where to start picking up the pieces. Carmella if I ever get my job back I am never going to look at another employee in a romantic way again. Kevin really fucked me over and for wait to pay for another semester of Law School. I said Amelio people like don't go far in life in life. Here is a good example today when I went to the gym I ran into this Blonde with big boobs in the locker room. When I was done with my workout the same blonde was in the locker room again, we both walked out of the locker room together and guess who was standing outside of the door....

Amelio wasn't in the mood to play the guessing game. Amelio who Sis who was at the door of the locker room Michael I told you he was no good... I said no not Michael, it was Joshua looking miserable as hell. The best part was when I introduced myself to her by telling her my name, she put her fucking head down and took a step back.... The bitch knew exactly who I was, can you believe that shit. Amelio that shit made my mind go crazy, I wanted to attack the both of them instead I kept my composer. I played the role of nothing went down like they were mutual friends. I asked so many questions oh and the best part is the bitch had the nerve to ask me if I wanted a ride home? Amelio asked what did you say to them? I told them no thank you my condo was only up the street on Tremont St. thank you for the offer and walked out of the gym, looking back when I was outside to see if I could see them they were gone....

Way to go Amelio said, it's about time you defended yourself from the way Joshua treated you I bet he is going through hell with this girl. I wish I could be as strong as you right now but I can't. I said I understand well I'm going to let you go I have a client in a few I have to finish getting ready. Okay Carmi be safe good night and be safe. You know I am always safe.... Amelio said I know you are thank you for picking up the phone tonight if you hadn't I wouldn't have spoken to you for a very long time. I know you would have I want you to know you are my little brother I won't do you wrong like that. You and Mom are the only people I have in this world….

Well I have to go call you later, yeah Sis call me later. When I looked at the time it was closer to Nine o'clock than I had thought. I was running late and the twins must be going crazy with their hard on… I had fifteen minutes to get to the Hotel, I Knew I was able to make it. I went downstairs I had Jerry call a cab for me, I hate having my clients wait for me. I was at the hotel within fifteen minutes, I was a few minutes late so I asked the woman at the front desk for the room the twins had reserved… the woman gave me one look up and down then told me where to go. Got on the elevator to the seventeenth floor, got to the front of the door when I arrived and knocked on it. The heavy accent came through the other side asking who is it? When the door opened I said hello Dajuan how are you tonight? I am good the man said yet I am Daothajuan. Well that is confusing, are you going to let me in. yes please come in the Daothajuan opened the door so I could come in.

I asked Daothajuan again when I walked into the room are you two ready for me? He said yes this time with a smile…. I said to the Daothajuan I have one request of the two of you, please take it easy on me the last time I was hired for my services I was in a pain for a long time. I don't want that to happen again. I could hear the shower running in the bathroom Dajuan was in there taking a shower. Daothajuan walked me over to the bed and began to undress me without warning. I said oh wait you have to pay before you get anything from me…. Now you know the price is double because it is the two of you. Daothajuan said yes yes in his very thick accent. Caramel we know the price and we have the money but I am ready for you right now….. Please come let me feel you. I didn't know what else to think they always had the money so I guess I could let it slide I told myself. At that moment I said okay what would you like for me to do for you? Just as I finished asking Daothajuan the question Dajuan came out of the bathroom naked with his penis hanging long and hard.

As twins they really shared everything and had no problem showing each other what they had. It was scary for two men, especially brothers to be that comfortable with each other, no matter how gay my brother is I would not show him my goodies. Other than that the I have no problem showing my body to my clients and Michael of course. I couldn't think of what these two men had in mind, I thought to myself I should have taken Michael's offer in tagging along he could have been my body guard, he would've protected me from any non-sense these twins would try to pull with me. Like always I had my blade.

Dajuan got close enough that I could feel the water dripping down his body, he and Daothajuan started to undress me by ripping off my clothes. I was liking the feeling of two men wanting me at the same time, my pussy got wet immediately I was ready for the freak fest that was about to happen with two African Mandingo Warriors. They sat me on the edge of the bed both standing in front of me naked. Having to use both his hands I began to caress their penises…. It was like holding two over sized hot dogs without the bun. I brought them closer to me as I opened my mouth to try to take in as much of their dicks as I could. I could hear them moaning as I moved from one penis to the other teasing the tip of their penises with my mouth. I used my tongue swiveling it around the tip of their penises one at a time. Dajuan being the bolder one grabbed t sides of my head and shoved his shaft inside of my mouth causing me to gag from the enormous pressure hitting the back of my throat; I liked the feeling.

I bopped my head back and forth a couple of times before Dajuan pulled me away from him and Daothajuan got closer for the same action. The African twins knew I used condoms so they had them on ready to go when I arrived. I could taste the strawberry flavor on it, not my favorite but it did just fine. Daothajuan was just as big as his brother just meatier in size. I grabbed his penis and inserted it inside of my mouth using my tongue to tickle the massive vein underneath his penis. I could hear Daothajuan grinding his teeth in pleasure. Daothajuan also moved away quickly, I scooted my now completely naked body to the middle of the king sized bed. I spread my legs apart as the twins bent down to putting there faces in my inner thighs using their tongues to finding their way up to my clitoris, my head cocked back as my body leaned forward I could feel their tongues taking turns swerving and sucking on my skin, it was the most amazing feeling to have two men pleasing me.

The twins then moved to each side of my body holding my legs apart;

Daothajuan was on the right side of my body sucking on my hard nipples, as Dajuan used his fingers to continue playing with my clitoris. It was amazing the way these two caressed my body with their fingers and tongue. I was ready for my African Warriors to put a hurting in places I didn't know existed on my body. The twins had gotten the condoms so I didn't have to worry about it. I went into my bag and pulled out the toys I had brought from the house. I knew I was dealing with the two Walla Walla Ding Dongs so I took out the vibrator ring which is place on the inner parts of the penis. I walked back to the bed where the twins were laying side by side rubbing themselves. I said who wants it first Dajuan raised his hand and said I do…. I walked over to Dajuan and placed the vibrator on his penis along with the magnum condom. Daothajuan still had the flavored condom on…. I opened my mouth as wide as I could and sucked his penis really hard. I could feel the condom slipping off with every time I sucked in. I put my knees on the bed, not taking my mouth off of Daothajuan's penis. I lifted my ass in the air insinuating to Dajuan to come join in. without hesitation Dajuan pulled my hips up to his level and shoved his super-sized penis into my vagina he gave it a few quick thrust before pulling and taking off the vibrator.

He went back in as I continued to suck on Daothajuan's dick with every thrust Daothajuan gave the harder I sucked on Dajuan's penis. Daothajuan's thrust became harder and quicker I could feel myself climaxing he had his hands in my hair helping me bop my head up and down on his brothers penis. Hmmm Hmm I gagged a bit before I let out a long moan. I had climaxed and was ready to switch the two around. I could see Dajuan's eyes roll to the back of his head he was ready to climax as well, I continued to suck on his penis. Daothajuan kept fucking me from behind, in just a few minutes I heard Daothajuan give out a long grunt as he tried to reach my stomach with his penis soon after Dajuan also climaxed.

My work was down within the hour and this time I didn't have to take the pain of having two men insert their enormous broom sticks inside of me…. Daothajuan stopped what he was doing and walked into the bathroom to remove the condom he had on. Dajuan removed it and placed it in the trash next to the bed. I asked for a towel to wipe myself down got dressed and waited for the money that was owe to me. Not only was I tired I was satisfied. Daothajuan came out of the bathroom as I got dressed and he went into his pant pocket and pulled out the money. What did these fool do rob a convenient store….. I grabbed the money and said call me if you need me again and walked out the door. I was tired now, I went down stairs waved a cab down and was on my way to get some sleep. What I thought was the end of my night was only the beginning…..

Chapter Seven

I got into the cab I had waved down, I told the driver where I was heading after the twins I was exhausted hungry and I just wanted to rest my eyes a bit. While I in the cab I noticed that Michael hadn't called me all night. He knew exactly where I was going to be and about what time I was getting home. I noticed the driver had arrived in front of my building in no time, when I looked at the meter I noticed he had charged me more than usual. I pulled out a twenty dollar from the money twenties I had in my purse and gave it to the driver telling him to keep the change. Before I could close the door of the cab the driver sped off. I walked into the building noticed that Jerry wasn't in his usual spot behind the desk; there was a young girl looking at a magazine and chewing gum…. I walked up to the girl to ask where was Jerry. The guard looked at me up and down still chewing on her gum she said I don't know I don't know I'm just covering his shift. I asked do you know when he's coming back. The guard shrugged her shoulders…. No I don't know with an attitude, still chewing on her gum.

I got the hint and made my way to the elevator. The guard stood up from the desk, she said in a loud tone UM EXCUSE WHERE DO YOU THINK YOUR GOING? You are suppose to sign in. I turned already frustrated and wanting to snatch the girl her collar, from behind the desk. I said I live her trying to keep my composer and not attacking the girl. I was tired of her shit I asked what is your name? the young girl said why do you want to know? I answered back with an attitude, so I could report your ass that's why…. I would not recommend that you work in this location again with your Ghetto Ass! I wasn't expecting the young girl to respond back for fear of losing her job, when she opened her mouth she said what ever I don't want to be in this snobby ass place with fake ass bitches like you. I was shocked that she would come back at me that way. I threw my hands up in the air and walked into the elevator not signing the visitors sheet that was laying on the desk with a pen beside it. The young girl still telling me I need to sign in I let the elevator door close and went up to my apartment fuck her she could sign it for me….

When I got off of the elevator I could feel my cell phone vibrating inside of my purse, I was trying to reach for my phone and the apartment keys at the same time that wasn't working. I was able to get to the keys because the phone had stopped vibrating as soon as I opened the door to my apartment, the phone began to vibrate again. I took the phone out of my purse I said HELLO…. It was Michael on the other line I could hear the loud music coming through the phone. Hey baby what are you doing did everything go smooth? I said yeah I just got home from one of my clients, still pissed off because of the guard downstairs I had to tell him about her… you know when I got home today the regular guard that is always there, well he is out tonight and the little bitch that is downstairs now just got on my last nerve, I really wanted to fight her. Michael said relax it's not worth it just relax… I'm still at the Casino with the Wicked Witch of Massachusetts until she decides to leave. I'm stuck here and wanted to come and see you just so I can have a taste of that sweet caramel candy.

I giggled loud enough that Michael could hear it, well after my clients today I will be on bed rest for the remainder of the night why don't you come by tomorrow like we had planned it. Michael said that's fine we can do that; have a good night and I will see you tomorrow. I said you too and drive home safe…. We ended the conversation at that, I was walking into my room to get my stuff ready for bed when I heard a loud knock at my door. I said hello who is it? The female voice on the other side of the door said it's the Police. I walked over to the peep hole to make sure that the young girl wasn't fucking around with my door. It was really the Police knocking at my door. I opened the door quick, I said hello officers is everything okay. There were two officers a female and a male officer the female did all the talking. The female said hello we are looking for Mrs. Carmella Ortega. I got nervous I said I'm she how can I help you at this time of night. The officer said we have been trying to reach you for the past two hours on behalf of your brother Amelio Ortega. I could feel my knees buckling at the thought of something happening to my brother.

My chest was caving in and my eyes began to water, I couldn't contain my emotions I asked what about my brother Amelio, the female officer looked at her partner then back at me…. She said ma'am we are sorry to inform you that your brother committed suicide late this afternoon. We need you to come down to identify the body. He is being held at the Hospital on Albany St., my mind wasn't complying with what the officer had told me. I said no not my brother I think you have the wrong person, I know he's going through some things with his job; he wouldn't commit suicide…. My tears were now rolling out of my eyes like a waterfall, down onto my face and on my clothes.

The female officer spoke as her partner stayed quiet and listened to everything she said. I looked at the both of them I knew Amelio would not do something like this, he was a professional lawyer just going through a rough time, he has worked so hard for what he had. Not my brother…. My mother has taught us to be stronger than that. The officer broke my trance when she asked me to go with them to make sure it was Amelio. I grabbed my purse and walked out of the apartment with the officers. We caught the elevator back down to the fist floor, when we got off the elevator the young security guard was no longer behind the desk, she was in the middle of the lobby looking around trying to figure out what was going on. Why were the Police there…. I had no time to deal with the non sense, when I walked past the guard I rolled my eyes and looked the other way as I made my way out of the building.

I walked outside of the building and looked up to see all the nosy neighbors looking out of their windows also trying to figure what is happening. The male officer said ma'am as he held the door to the back seat of the cruiser. After closing my door the officer jumped into the passenger seat. The female officer was driving she put her lights on and did drove off since Tremont St. was a one way it was easy for her to pull out. We were on our way to the Hospital where Amelio's body was being held, the thought of that alone sent chills down my spine. My mind was going crazy I have to call my mother and give her the bad news about her son, I would have to explain how we've been living our lives. It is going to break her heart to find out all the sins that Amelio and I have committed…. Poor Amelio he must've really liked this guy to go as far as committing suicide. I needed to be there for him and I wasn't, oh god what am I going to tell my mother…..

The police cruiser stopped in front of the Beige building it was the City Morgue which was right next to the hospital. The officer opened the back door to let me out, my nerves told my knees not to move, I couldn't go any further. My mind was telling my body to move, yet my body refused to listen…. The male officer grabbed my elbow and helped me out of the cruiser and into the City Morgue. They led me to the far end of the hall where there were several doors. The thoughts of me and Amelio playing at the beach together when we went to Puerto Rico…. The way I used him as my make up dummy when I took classes in cosmetology the thoughts rushed into my mind like a flashback causing my tears to rush down faster with every step I closer to where Amelio's body was found. I finally arrived at the room, I walked to see the body laying on the gurney with the traditional white blanket over it. I was not ready to ready to see this, I was not ready to see my brother lying on the gurney. I was use to seeing my brother cheerful living life. Even though he's had a rough few weeks he was alive.

My knees couldn't take my weight anymore, the officers held me up as the gentleman inside of the room revealed the body to me. I couldn't believe it…. I said OH MY GOD OH MY GOD, this is a joke right. I was crying harder, I fell to my knees the officers

72

helped me up. The female officer apologized then said I have to ask you is this the body of Amelio Ortega? In one quick answer I said NO! everyone in the room looked at each other. The female officer focused her eyes back on me... Ms. Ortega are you sure this is not your brother. With tears in my eyes I said yes I'm sure I know what my brother looks like and that is not my brother. That man's name is Keith, no it's Kevin. He had a fling with my brother that got Amelio in trouble at work with a law suit. I asked the officers are you sure he was at my brothers house? The officers took me out of the room while the gentleman that was there covered the body back up. We were walking out of the City Morgue, I noticed the officers looking at each other. The female officer pulled out her cell phone then walked to a corner to have a private chat.... The male officer stood by my side making sure I wouldn't leave. The female officer hung up the cell phone then walked back towards me and her partner.

Ms. Ortega I have to bring you to the police station for questioning... we need to find out what's going on. This just turned into a Homicide case and your brother Amelio is the main suspect. If you know where he is you need to tell us. The relief I had gotten that Amelio was still alive went that fast, now I had to worry about what has Amelio gotten himself into. Did he really kill this guy was it worth it? The two officers escorted me back to the cruiser where we all got in and headed to the police department where I was going to answer a lot of questions I didn't have the answers to. All I wanted was for my body to rest, I wanted to call Amelio and ask him what the fuck was going on.... First things first I needed to go with these officers and answer the questions their boss had for me. I sat in the police cruiser thinking where could he be at? How could he disappear after doing this shit to Kevin.

Has he lost his mind, now he's dragging me into his mess. The cruiser had stopped in front of a building that read Police Department in yellow letters with their insignia at the bottom of the letters. We had gotten there quicker than I thought it would take.... The officer let me out of the cruiser, then led me into the opal colored building. My heart was racing faster than normal. We went past the entrance through the metal detectors, I placed my purse on the belt forgetting I had the knife in there. It went through the scanner undetected I was relieved. We walked down the quick almost empty building down a hall, I picked up my paced to catch up with the female officer who seemed non chalant.... I asked in a low voice what's going on? What's going to happen now? The officer said the detective in charge of this case is going to ask you a few questions answer them honestly, when everything is said and done Officer Cruz and I will escort you back home.

I said I don't know what's going on I just want to get to the bottom of this myself. I know my brother and he wouldn't do such a thing. The officer looked at me then said no matter how much you think you know a person you really don't know them unless you're a mind reader. On that note I stayed quiet and continued to walk by her side.... We walked down the hall, I noticed the black gentleman walking towards us. He said hello Mrs. Ortega I am Detective Jones I have some questions for you about the young mans body inside of the morgue. They will consist of how you know him, where you met him things like that.... I need you to be honest with me, its late and we all want to go home. If I think your lying to me the process will take longer. I nodded my head as the detective continued talking. Mrs. Ortega can you help us figure out what is going on. My mind began to wonder again where is Michael when I need him the most.

Though we are just friends this is the time to show me if he is truly interested in me and not playing games. We walked up to the door on the side of the hall; the detective opened the door he said after you, and please have a seat. He told the officers to wait outside then closed the door behind him. The room had a desk and plaques all around hanging on the walls I thought I would be in a room with a two way mirror like the movies, it didn't.... the detective took a seat behind the desk. Opened up the desk drawer and pulled out a digital recorder, Detective Jones pressed the ON button on the recorder and began to talk into it. He said his name, then mine and asked if I gie him permission to record me. I said yes I Carmella Ortega give permission to I looked at the plaques on the walls to get the detective's full name, when I got the full name I said I give

Detective Derek Jones permission to record this interrogation.... The detective nodded his head then said Mrs. Ortega, I correctly him quickly, I said I'm not married and I don't have children its miss.... The detective apologized for his mistake then continued, with the questions the first one was do you know the whereabouts of your brother Amelio Ortega? I said no... have you spoken to your brother lately? Yes this evening before leaving the house. The detective continued by asking me if I knew the man that was found in your brother's house? I said I met him once at a night club in Rhode Island, he and my brother were flirting with each other that night.... The detective kept asking me questions about Amelio his mental health, his Profession, and his sexuality. I answered all the questions I could before he decided to let me leave. When I looked at the clock on the wall it read damn near three in the morning. I was done I couldn't answer anymore questions.

When the interrogation was over the detective got up from his seat and walked to the door and opened it. The two officers were still sitting outside of the office, I walked out of the office. Before I was completely out of the door the detective stopped me then said, I believe you don't know where your brother is but if you get in contact with him please have him turn himself in, it would be easier that way.... I nodded my head and kept walking out of the office, I was tired, my mind was going crazy I didn't know what was the next step in finding Amelio. Detective Jones told the two officers we are all done here, take her home please....it was finally over for just one night. The officers walked me back out to the cruiser and again we got inside, I was driven back home. I was in front of the building quickly, I thanked the officers and walked inside. Once inside of the building the young guard was still sitting behind the desk with a big as grin on her face. I was waiting for her to say something out of the ordinary, so I could jump on her ass... I looked at her hard, rolled my eyes and kept walking towards the elevator. I pressed the button for the elevator to come down, when it got to the first floor I got in and went up to my apartment I was on my way to bed.

I had a long night and in the afternoon I had a lot of things to do, I had to find Amelio, find out what exactly was going on, why would he leave a man hanging in his house like that…. Has he lost his mind? I spoke to him yesterday and he sounded fine over the phone, maybe it time for me to be a big sister and start paying attention to him. I got in front of my apartment door and pulled out the keys, I gave out a big sigh I was finally home. Without thinking twice I walked into the apartment and straight to my bedroom I jumped on my bed getting some sleep was my first priority everything else will be taken care of when I wake up in the afternoon… I was still boggled as to how did my life get so complicated to the point where the law enforcement had to get involved. I thought to myself why is this happening? WHY! I went to bed within seconds my eyes were shut I was quickly drifting into my dream world, a place where nothing or no one would disturb me so I thought….

My sleep was interrupted by the night mares of Kevin's body on the Gurney at the hospital, when the covers were pulled back instead of seeing Kevin I would see Amelio. I would walk closer to the body and see his eyes prop open…. Then his mouth would move he kept saying "NOT EVERYONE IS TRUSTWORTHY." The sentence alone would scare me out of my sleep, ending the dream…. I went through the whole morning repeating the same dream over and over again it was driving me crazy and I couldn't take it anymore. I finally woke up around twelve noon. I went into the bathroom to wash up; I had a long day ahead of me. I needed to take care of some business that couldn't wait. The first thing on my agenda was finding Amelio…. I jumped into the shower and scrubbed the scent of Dajuan and Daothajuan off of me. Have that smell on me was over bearing I smelt like the jungle versus Egypt. They went over board with the oils. I love the oils from the carts in the plaza, my thing is knowing when and how much to use. These guys took a bath in the oils; I think they could've use the whole bottle.

I was done in the shower, grabbed the towel to wrap myself in and was getting ready to brush my teeth when my cell phone began to ring. I ran out of the bathroom knocking over the laundry bag that I had next to the door. I was able to catch the call on the last ring. I said hello Amelio…. The voice on the other line said no Michael. I said hey baby what's going on. Michael must have heard the concern on my voice he asked was everything alright you sound out of breath…. I said I was in the shower when you called I thought it was Amelio, I need to find him and quick. He got himself in some trouble, I had the police in my house and I had to go look at a dead person…. To top it off I had to go to the Police Station to answer questions about my brother. It was a crazy night Michael…. Michael said wow that is a crazy night, well I'm still at the Casino with the Wicked Witch.

I think she is ready to leave so I'll be down in a few hours if you need anything. I said no I just need to get dressed and find my brother,this shit is big. I hope he is okay where ever he is at. Michael said I hope you find him, I need help with something myself but I guess it's going to have to wait. I feel like I have Blue Balls and it hurts. I laughed to myself I said right now I need to finish what I had planned on doing for the day and if I have any time you know I would be more than excited to help you relieve some of that tension that you have built up…. Michael gave a small chuckle, I could hear the female in the background telling Michael she was ready to go. Michael said I got to let you go, call you when I'm back in Boston…. I said okay then ended the phone conversation with Michael.

I went back inside of the bathroom to finish brushing my teeth and getting dressed, I brushed my hair into a bun; I was so exhausted from the night before I didn't put on any make-up I just kept it casual. I made sure I had everything I needed before I headed out of my apartment. I went down to the lobby, the young girl that was there the entire night was gone…. Now there was an older man about Jerry's age he said Good Afternoon miss how are you today? I said fine thank you and yourself? Good the man answered back, before I walked out of the door I asked is Jerry okay, I was trying to ask the young girl that was here last night but her attitude got in the way. The guard chuckled he said I noticed…. These young bucks all have attitudes no offense to you. I said non taken…. As for Jerry his wife said he had a Heart Attack a few days ago after work while he was at home, if it wasn't for their dog he wouldn't have made it. It's true what is said about a dog being a man's best friend. I said wow well if you hear from his wife please find out where Jerry is hospitalized, he is well loved in this building we can send him get well gifts…. The guard said I will speak to my supervisor and see what they say.

I said thank you and again have a good afternoon, I waved my hand and walked out of the double doors. I thought to myself wow Jerry had a Heart Attack he seemed so strong and yet his heart was so weak. I needed to worry about other things and finding Amelio. The first place I was going to was to his office to talk to Tina his secretary to see if she has seen or spoken to Amelio. Then I have to call my mother and tell her everything that is going on, she is not going to be happy about it…. What the hell is going on I can't believe this shit is really happening, I need to go to the gym and relieve some stress. I know that's not happening right.

I waited for the public bus in front of the Commons, when it arrived I paid my fare then walked to the back of the bus. I was on the bus when I felt my phone vibrating inside of my Tote Bag. I quickly took a look at the Caller ID it was Amelio, I answered the phone….. Where the fuck are you? Everyone on the bus looked back to stare at me, then went on about their business. Amelio said hey Sis I love you too. I said no Amelio this is no time to joke you have the Boston Police looking for your ass. I had to talk to a Detective that asked me all these questions about you. Amelio said why I haven't done anything I'm in Puerto Rico with Mom. Ive been here for two days now…. I said yeah well let me in on a little secret, if you don't turn yourself in you will be in a lot more trouble then you are now. They found Kevin's body inside of your house dead, like I sad you are in a lot of trouble and the detectives think you did it. Since no could find you or contact you they're blaming you, making you the main suspect. You need to cut your vacation short and come handle this shit.

Amelio stayed quiet, then breaking the silence he said I didn't kill anyone those Mother Fuckers are out of their minds. Sis I need you to do me a favor don't tell anyone where I'm at, I will be on the next plane back to Boston. I told mom everything about my sexuality and now I have to tell her that I am being accused of Murder…. Damn will I ever get a break? Amelio went from feeling relieved to having to deal with something else in just a matter of weeks. I could hear the frustration in his voice. I said I'm on my way to your office to see if Tina had seen you. Amelio cut me off he said no, don't go there instead go to my house and call me when you get there alright…. I said I won't get in trouble for going there will I. Amelio said no you won't just call me when you get there alright. I said okay just hurry back to Boston. We hung up, I loved my brother very much now it's time for me to step up and give him the help he's been asking for so long.

I stayed on the bus to Dudley and got on the a different Bus to Mattapan, which left me a block from Amelio's house. It took about forty-five minutes to get there, I thought to myself if Michael were here he would have driven me without no doubt. When I got to Amelio's house I looked around to see if the Police were around, I didn't see any so I call Amelio I told him where I was at. He said I need you to go inside of the house and grab a camcorder that I have inside of the mattress. I said they found that, Amelio said no they didn't because I had sewn it inside of the mattress. Just go upstairs and grab the camcorder, I hung up the phone and started towards the house.

Before I could make it to the front of the house one of Amelio's neighbors was in my face, she said I saw everything your gay ass brother is in a lot of trouble. That' s what happens when you commit sins against God…. He leaves you either to repent or to the Demons. I said to the lady let me guess the gates will always be open to you because you are a good Christian woman. The lady nodded her head. I said well I guess I will be going to hell too because I think you are a nosy bitch who needs to get fucked in order to keep you away from that window. The woman looked at me surprised at what I said. I said and if you don't get away from me I will cut you. The woman grunted then walked away without saying another word. She stopped to talk to another woman that was sitting on the porch of the house next door to Amelio's. I ignored the both of them as they whispered to each other. I walked to the house, went inside since the door already opened they destroyed Amelio's house what ever he had the police took it or it was stolen by the crack heads of this neighborhood.

I went upstairs to his bedroom took the bed spread off of the and saw what a shitty job Amelio did with the sewing. I don't know how the police over looked this…. Any was I took my knife out and cut where the stitches were, when I looked there was the camcorder, I grabbed it and shoved it inside of my tote bag…. I couldn't take the smell of blood any more I left out of the house as fast as I could without looking back. I walked back to the bus stop waited about ten minutes and did the same process of getting back home. It took another forty-five minutes to get home, I got off the bus when it arrived in front of the Commons again and walked the rest of the way home. I ran across the street not looking to see if any cars were coming. I went into the double doors, and inside of my complex. Once I was inside, I noticed that Michael was standing in the lobby area with a bottle of Moscato and flowers in his hand. I smiled and said hey what are you doing here. Michael said I couldn't wait anymore I had to see you and taste you. I said well I'm a bit tired, Michael said you don't have to worry about a thing I will do all the work I know you had a long night and now it's time for me to take care. I giggled then said come on lets go upstairs. Michael followed me to the elevator I took the flowers out of his hands a he pressed for the elevator it was already there we went up to relax….

Chapter Eight

Michael and I arrived upstairs in my apartment, still with the camcorder in my tote bag I said Michael go have a seat I will be right with you. Michael said how about I take a shower since I was inside of that smelly Casino all night and I could smell the wicked witch perfume all over me. I said okay towels are in the linen closet and if you need anything else just let me know I will get it for you. Michael said there is something I do need come inside of the bathroom so I can show you what I'm talking about. Michael looked at me with a flirtatious smile on his face. I said okay you go in first I will follow you in a few seconds. Michael said okay. When Michael walked into the bathroom I quickly took the camcorder out and went to hide it in the safe until Amelio got back into Boston. I found out where Amelio was at and know I'm going to satisfy Michael to the point where he will pass out. After putting the camcorder inside of the safe I walked inside of the bathroom to Michael who was already in the shower. I took off my clothes then slid into the shower behind Michael. I said hey stranger lets see how much tension you have down in that section. I took my hands and rubbed his back I could hear Michael moaning as I took the soap into my hands and with the wash cloth began to caress that one part of his body that grew to it's enormous size.

I said that was a quick erection, Michael said yeah he misses you now that you're here touching him he is excited and ready to play with his playmate. I giggled then said why don't you turn around so he can see the new hair cut his playmate got just for him. When Michael turned around he began to laugh, I got it done two days ago and instead of going commando I had Phil make an arrow pointing down to the spot. Michael said well I think he likes it very much because he is poking the hell out of trying to get inside, and she's not letting him. I said well Michael let's finish taking the smell of cheap perfume off you so we can get the rest of our night started. Michael said you are absolutely right he quickly washed himself and me then grabbed my hand I almost fell to the ground but Michael was there to grab me. We rushed into the bedroom where Michael came up from behind to tossed me on the bed, the only thing that came out of me was a squeal. Then I felt Michael spread my legs apart, he quickly dove his face into my inner thighs tasting everything that dripped from my vagina. His tongue wiggling in every direction it could. Could feel his tongue entering and exiting my vagina with force pushing up against my clitoris. My body curved to the feeling of his tongues movement. Michael stopped abruptly then moved his head upward towards my chin using his tongue to lick the wet spots left by the shower. Without hesitation Michael jammed his Mandingo penis inside of me. It was amazing the way he moved his hips in circular motions, I felt the pleasure I did not feel with my clients.

Michael took his right hand and squeezed my breast as he continued to thrust my vagina. YEAH BABY …. MAKE IT CUM. I could hear myself as Michael thrust got harder and faster he was hitting my G-spot and it was feeling real good. He stopped then flipped me over on my stomach I was starting to get on my knees when Michael said no just stay like that…. He began to rub my back down to my ass cheeks when he reached the crack of my ass he spread my legs apart again, Michael again dove right in I could feel his wet tongue move from my vagina to my ass and back to my vagina, it was feeling real good I had never felt that in my years as an escort. Within minutes I had climaxed all over Michael's face and he was enjoying it. Michael grabbed my waist to lift me up, when he got me to the level he wanted me at he began to thrust his penis into my vagina pounding on my vagina like it was the last one on the planet.... I could feel his sweat dripping from his succulent body it made me climax one more time.

Right after I climaxed Michael let out his first climax of the night. He quickly threw himself on the bed then let me know he was missing me a lot this week. I told him I missed him too. Michael started something in me that only he could relieve, he laid on the bed as I got up to wipe myself off... I said I got something special for you just stay lying on the bed. Michael said okay, I walked into the bathroom to get the oils I buy off the carts in the Downtown area. As I walked back to the room I could hear Michael snoring on the bed, within the minutes I had walked into the bathroom and to the room he had fallen asleep. He must have been really tired, I placed the oils on the night stand and laid next to him... Michael opened his eyes and said hey baby are you tired? I said no but I know you are. I could hear you snoring when I walked inside of the room, what did that bitch do to you? Keep you up all night. Michael said yeah and she had me going from one Casino to the next as she blew through her husbands money. It was driving me crazy, when she finally decided to leave it was about one in the afternoon.

I said yeah that was a crazy day baby go on and sleep, I know you're tired. Michael said yeah I am. We closed our eyes and went to sleep, when we woke up the first thing I asked Michael was are you hungry? Michael said yeah what do you want to eat? I said I could go for some Crab Ragoons.... Michael said yeah I could go for sum yung cuticat. I began to laugh I never heard that one before. I said seriously what do you want to eat? Michael said why not get a PUPU Platter for two, that way we can both have what we want. Then I will some Caramel for dessert. I thought that was the cheesiest line I have ever heard come out of Michael's lips. Though I played along with his flirting.... I said well this Caramel has something for you to taste and it's sweet and juicy. Michael looked at me then said go on girl order the food and ask for steamed rice not fried. I asked you don't eat fried rice Michael responded there is something about the brown rice that turns me off. I said that is too funny, I thought Amelio was the only one that didn't eat fried rice. Amelio oh shit I forgot about him, I quickly got up to check my cell phone to see if Amelio had called.

When I flipped the phone open I saw that I had one voice message and a missed call from Amelio. I pressed the send button to call Amelio back. I could hear him in the other line talking loud like he wanted everyone to hear what he was saying. He said Carmella what's going on I told you I would call as soon as I got back into town. I said where are you know? Amelio said in jail they had to arrest me for the murder of Kevin Spritzer. I said who? Amelio said Kevin that was his last name…. I said well that's a fucked up last name. Amelio was getting agitated with me, Carmella focus Amelio said I need you to come bail me out. Okay baby brother how much is the bail? Amelio answered thirty thousand dollars. WHAT ! I replied Thirty Thousand dollars to bail you out…. Amelio said Sis I will pay you back. Once I get out of here. I said okay Amelio I am going to pay the bail I'm on my way…. No Carmella you have to come on Monday because it's the weekend I have to spend the weekend in here. to wait to be seen by the Judge, I just used Thirty thousand as an example. Okay Amelio where am I going to bring the money to on Monday? I don't know yet Carmella but I will let you know when Monday comes pay attention to your phone. Yeah I will, let me let you go I have to order food for Michael he's hungry. Carmella remember to answer you phone and where is the camcorder? Amelio it's in a safe place and how is it that you're still using your cell pone, don't they take it away when you get arrested….. Yeah they do, the officers know me in here so they're being lenient with me.

Okay well you take care of your self in there and I will see you on Monday. I closed the phone then re-opened it, I dialed the number for the Chinese Restaurant to place the order for the food. When I went back into the bedroom Michael was still laying on the bed. Hey Hon, what did you want again? Michael said I want a PUPU Platter for two and some steamed rice, not fried. I get it smart ass, Michael chuckled then patted the bed for me to join him. I jumped on the bed then pressed the speed dial for the Chinese restaurant, when the Asian man answered the phone I placed the order of the PUPU platter and two colas. Michael looked at me, what if I wanted something other than cola to drink what if I just wanted juice? Michael I know you and you would not like the juices they have. Okay I rust you.

After I ordered the food, I got on top of Michael. Well since you did all the work earlier and we have about forty five minutes to work up an appetite before the food arrives how about I show you what I can really do? Michael looked at me with a big grin on his face, I felt his penis rise for the second time this night. Michael why don't you close your eyes and this time do not go to sleep on me. Okay Carmella I promised just don't stick something up my ass, I would have to fight a woman for the first time in my life. I laughed as I grabbed the oils off the night stand. Michael laid there with all his clothes off; are you ready? I could see his Mandingo penis looking as tall as the Empire State building. I got closer to Michael this will feel a bit cold at the beginning and then it will heat up…. Michael asked what is it? You will find out just relax your mind and like I said let me do all the work this time. Michael closed his eyes for the third time.

I poured the exotic oils into my hand I placed the bottle back on the night stand then rubbed my hands together. I gently placed my hands on Michael's penis he squirmed a bit, then he had a quick shiver. I moved my hands up and down giving Michael a slow hand job, Michael said your right it is cold yet now it's starting to warm up what is that? Shhhh don't talk I moved my hands to hold his penis as I used my tongue to lick the tip of Michael's penis like the professional I am. I could hear Michael moaning and wiggling…. I tried to stuff Michael's penis deep into my throat, I gagged a couple of times, then kept going. Hmm baby that feels oh I could feel the reaction as I started to suck on his penis harder. Ah, I jumped up did I hurt you? Michael said no, it just feels real good please don't stop. I went back in to suck on his penis some more. Michael said give me some of that candy you have, I want to taste some more of it.

We were now doing the Sixty nine position with me on the top. The faster Michael used his tongue the harder I sucked on his penis until our climax met. We both climaxed together it was out of this world, not even with Joshua have I ever felt and explosion in my body like that. My body jerked every which way as Michael continued to suck in all the juices from my body, making sure he indulged in all the juice that flowed out of me. Stop I can't take it any more. Michael took one last slurp before moving his head away from my inner thighs. Wow that was great… I think you worked me for one day, Michael looked at me I don't think that is possible, no disrespect but with your profession I really didn't think that was possible. Well even with my profession my vagina is not bionic it still needs a break once and a while. Michael laughed at the comment I had made, he said you're right I should know better. He continued to move away from me as we positioned ourselves the correct way on the bed. Do you hear that? I propped up on the bed, yeah that's just the buzzer the Chinese food is here.

We both got up from the bed and got dressed then we walked into the living room to get the money out of my purse. Before I could pull the money out of my purse Michael had his wallet in one hand and was handing me the money with the other… the buzzer continued to ring wow that delivery man is impatient let him in before he does something to our food. The delivery man was at the door within minutes knocking on the door. I walked over to the door with the money in hand and opened it…. Surprise, surprise Joshua what the hell are you doing here? Joshua looked just as surprised, I'm delivering some food. I could tell that it was killing him inside to have me seeing him like this after what he did to me when how abandoned me leaving me with nothing but my clothes and health. Wow you have gone to your lowest… and you have gotten to your highest Joshua replied I can't believe that someone as lazy as you could afford a place like this. I noticed he was looking over my shoulder when I turned to see Michael standing behind me, listening to everything.

Michael came closer to the door, hey baby is there a problem? I gave Joshua the two twenty dollar bills I had in my hand, keep the change you'll need it for Sammy…. I said hey Joshua how is your girlfriend? I haven't seen her in the gym… Joshua looked at me then said she's in the Bahamas on a photo shoot. I said oh so she's a model, Michael looked at me baby that's none of your business come on let's go eat. I said you're right its none of my business I closed the door as Joshua rolled his eyes and turned to walk back to the elevator. Michael and I walked to the kitchen, before I could say anything Michael was questioning me about Joshua…. Who was that one of your clients? No he was never my client, I looked at Michael that was Joshua the one that took everything away from me… Ooh Michael replied; yeah he was the one that had me playing wife and never married me, the one that played me like a piano, guitar, Violin whatever instrument you can easily get rid of when you're tired of it. I had to go live with Amelio then I started this business, well you know what I mean. Michael looked at me as I kept talking on and on.

Joshua put me through so much now look at him delivering food just to make his miss perfect happy. He got her a boob job, whatever she wants he gets it for her and when it was me I had to do whatever he said in order to get something in return. Oh well just like I told him when Joshua walked out the door that girl was going to juice him for everything he got, and that's exactly what is happening. I could see that Michael was feeling a bit uncomfortable so I walked over to him and swung my arms around his neck in a soft tone I whispered well all I have to think about right now is you and this appetite you helped me work up. Michael chuckled lets eat I already have the plates set, and I don't want to eat cold rice. Michael pulled out the barstool for me… Michael pulled out the other barstool and sat down next to me. I still had a lot to do in the morning Amelio being my first priority. I figured out a plan in my head as Michael got comfortable on the bed… hey Michael I can't believe that Joshua is delivering food after everything he put me through you know what were his last words to me, "when I get my shit together to give him a call." Joshua told me that right before he walked out of the door. Michael said wow that's harsh…. Yeah and when I saw him at the gym a few weeks ago he look so miserable; now see why, the girl has been juicing him for his money, and he is so hooked on the girl that he's not seeing what she is doing to him.

Carmella then why are you so worried about him, he did you wrong the girl he left you for is playing him he's getting what he deserves… yet it sounds to me like you still have feelings for the man. No Michael I don't have feelings for the man, I just can't believe that he was so different with me and look how it turned out for Joshua. Don't worry he will notice it sooner or later what models are about, Carmella you only need to worry about you and come back to bed…. Your right Michael I'm coming back to bed and Joshua is getting everything he deserves. Michael chuckled then grabbed me by the waist dragging me back into the bed, it was fun and sexy at the same time. Michael began to tickle me, I couldn't help it at Three O'clock in the morning I was laughing so loud I thought I was going to wake the neighbors. Michael you need to stop the neighbors are going to complain about the noise. Michael said your right lets go to bed.. I said yeah lets go to bed I have to bail Amelio out on Monday and I'm not looking forward for it. Michael said oh okay then you need to go to bed and get lots of rest, Carmella if you need a ride I can take you. We'll see but right now its time for bed, yeah your right its time for bed…. We both got comfortable under the blanket, I closed my eyes feeling relaxed in Michael's arms.

Chapter Nine

It was nine thirty in the morning when Michael and I woke up. I was amazed that he has been spending a lot of time with me knowing my occupation has not scarred him away at all. I figured he would have used me for something and bounced after he got what he needed. He has not done any of that even though last night was awkward with the whole Joshua being the delivery guy. Michael has been a wonderful caring man though we're not in a relationship it feels like it… there might be a possibility of there being one. I can't imagine what it will turn out to be like. Will I give myself to him completely like I did with Joshua or will I hold back so I won't get hurt in the long run? I was deep in thought when I felt something poke me on my ass. It was Michael, early in the morning he was poking me with his MANDINGO SNAKE…. I couldn't help it I responded to what Michael was asking of me without words. I said honey you're ready so early in the morning, how could I not take advantage of being able to wake up next to a beautiful woman and not have this sensation to have her. I turned to look at Michaels big brown eye, I love the way his lashes over lapped giving Michael the innocent look.

I said you have beautiful eye's they make me wonder how much of a mystery you can be. Michael looked at me then he winked his eye and said well if you look under the covers you will see that I am not a mystery at all. Instead I will tell you every thing that is needed to be known of me…. Like right now what's on my mind is getting inside of you and wiggling around to see if I could find your pelvic. I laughed hard at the comment Michael had made, it even made my vagina feel like a waterfall of wetness. I began to think will Michael be able to go that deep inside of me? At least that far? I jumped on Michael then slowly wiggled my wet pussy onto his penis. I said well lets see how deep inside of me you can get? Michael grabbed me y the waist and pulled me down onto his hard penis. Ah I felt his penis penetrate me, after the pain came the pleasure I wined my body from left to right making sure Michael could feel the walls of my vagina. I could hear Michael moaning, if I open my eyes to look at him I will climaxed to soon. Think of sweet tasting candy. I was not Carmella with all the worries on top of this man, I was Caramel giving Michael a morning treat.

Michael placed his hands on my ass cheeks, he began pumping up and down really quick. Aww it felt like his penis was slamming into the top if my stomach. I could hear Michael saying, RIDE IT HARD YEAH THAT'S IT… Oh my goodness Michael was hitting my G spot in the perfect place. I could feel my vagina contracting in and out. When I finally decided to open my eyes Michael gave me a look that sent me into complete ecstasy. My body became very tense as I climaxed all over Michaels penis , I could not stop it. It felt so strong my clitoris tightened as I as I let loose of all of my juices. Soon after I climaxed Michael started to thrust harder and faster, within minutes Michael gave out a loud grunt then closed his eyes as tight as he could and without realizing it squealed like a little girl. I stopped pumping my ass when I heard Michael make that noise. I said what the hell was that? Michael said I climaxed, that was really really good. I said I'm not talking about climaxing.

I'm talking about the girly noise you made at the end. Michael looked at me, he said I didn't make a girly noise. I laughed still sitting on top of Michael. I said that was a girl sound to me. Michael said with a grin on his face whatever then pushed me off from on top of him. Jokingly I copied the noise that he had made when he climaxed. Michael said so you have jokes? Well here's a funny one, I'm not the one thinking of sweet candy just so I won't climax early. I looked at Michael, then hitting him gently with a pillow I told Michael I don't do that, knowing very well I do. Michael looked at me, I said okay I didn't think I did it out loud. I giggled as I made my way out of the bed.

Well I'm going to take a shower if you want to join me. Michael nodded his head as he climbed out of the bed, along with me. We both made our way to the bathroom when my phone rang....only two people call me on the house phone, my mother and Amelio. I answered the phone quick... hello, hey the voice on the other line was depressed, it's me your brother Amelio, can you come get me the hell out of here? I hate it, it's disgusting I feel and smell nasty and the judge already gave me the a bail of twenty five thousand, only because she knew me. Okay Amelio I'm getting ready now, I have to run to the bank, hoping Amelio will catch on to what I was saying. I said I have to withdraw the money and then go down there. Amelio was the only one that knew about the safe I kept inside of the apartment. When I told him I had to run to the bank Amelio went bonkers, telling me how much he hates it in there that I needed to hurry up, why was I going to the bank when I have the money in the house. I tried to cut him off but he was talking too much that the phone automatically cut off in the middle of his complaining.

When I looked back Michael was standing at the bathroom door, your brother is a dangerous man when he is upset. Yeah I know. Michael said I heard everything and if you were trying to keep it a secret it didn't work. Michael turned to walk back into the bathroom, he said it's dangerous to keep a safe inside of your apartment. You should know better.... I looked at Michael you didn't know I had a safe in the apartment until you ease dropped on my conversation with Amelio. I couldn't tell what had gotten into Michael, by the look on his face and the giant steps he was taking I thought the worse, his facial expression was serious angry, and agitated at the same time. Michael grabbed me by my arms and brought me close to his body, in a strong tone Michael said.... ARE YOU STUPID? My body popped as he moved me away from his body. I looked at Michael he could see that I was scared, and he was hurting me. Michael lowered his tone and loosened his grip on my arms. Michael said if I wanted to robbed you I would have done it the first time you let me into your apartment. I know where your safe is I noticed it when I first came in here, that was the very first night I could have robbed you then. I said prove it still in doubt that he knew where the safe was. By the facial expression I knew Michael was getting agitated, Michael shook his head, he placed his hand on the middle of my back and said come on lets go into the living room so I can prove it to you. You want me to prove it to you fine I will show you where your safe is.

In a sarcastic way I said where the hell do you think your going? Michael fired back I'm proving to you the obvious. We both walked into the living room. Before we were completely in the living room I said okay you know where the safe is. Michael said baby I just want you to see how dangerous it is to have a safe in your apartment. Michael apologized I didn't mean to hurt you. Michael continued what if it wasn't me and it was one of your clients a loser a really big loser, the man could easily beat you up, force you to open the safe that inside of the wall behind the frame just above the bar take whatever is inside of it and leave you for dead, or beaten half to death. If it were me I would leave you dead so you wouldn't be able to identify me. I looked at Michael dumb founded the fact he knew exactly where the safe was… I didn't know it was that obvious. I asked Michael how could you tell the safe is in the wall? Michael looked at me, well if you look at the frame its not hugging the wall like frames are suppose too.

Michael continued to tell how there was a gap between the wall and the frame, which means there is something behind it. I had to muster up the courage to admit that he was right…. I said okay your right you didn't have to get upset about it. Michael came close to me, gave me a bear hug so tight that I could barely breath I could feel the muscles on his six pack stomach. Then he said softly in my ear I'm sorry it won't happen again, I want you to be safe that's all. He continued to talk as he held me in his arms, it's okay Michael I care about you too. And if you ever grab me like that again I will rip your balls off. Michael pushed me away and gently rubbed himself …. That sounds painful. Teasing I said of course it will be painful I will make sure of it. Michael said I won't try you any more, now how about that shower. Yeah lets go take a shower and save my brother before he really loses his mind. Michael looked at me, we both walked back to the bathroom. Michael pretended to act like Amelio and the Diva that he was. Imagine he wants to get out I would think he would like that he is in a cell full of men.

After getting ready Michael and I went to free Amelio out of the Hadley Correctional Facility in other word the jail Amelio was being held at. Having so much money on me and not being able to spend it was not fun at all, it was actually burning a hole in my pocket. It took fifteen minutes to get to the jail from my apartment, I lived so close to the jail and never knew it existed. We went inside of the building both Michael and I looked for signs that led to where I had to pay for Amelio's bail. When we couldn't find it we asked the first person that had walked past us. The person told us where to go to pay Amelio's bail, it wasn't in the same building. By the time we finished with everything it was close to two thirty in the afternoon. When Amelio actually got out of the building he got on his hands and knees and was kissing the floor, or at least pretending to kiss the floor. Amelio ran over to me and gave me a hug, like he hasn't seen me in years.

Amelio, I had to pry him off of me, can you stop acting so dramatic… let's get the hell out of here I'm hungry and want to see what's on the camcorder. I repeated myself I want to see what's on the camcorder that is going to save your ass from going to jail for the rest of your life. Amelio asked did you bring it with you? I said yes I did now get in the car so we could go eat. As Amelio was opening the car door a young white girl came up to Amelio she was very thin with a lot of hips shapely I would say. She asked are you Amelio? Amelio said with attitude yes I am who… before Amelio could finish the sentence the girl cocked her fist and punched Amelio in the face. I got back out of the car as the girl yelled out profanity to Amelio…. You gay mother fucker, because you couldn't have my husband you killed him. Your going straight to hell where you will burn for what you did to me and my husband. Amelio was shocked at what just happened, when he realized it he was bleeding out of his nose. Michael got out of the car and made his way to where we were all standing on the side walk. Amelio lunged at the young girl to attack her. Michael was quick enough to stop Amelio before he could put his hands on her. Even though Amelio is gay he was still a man, and he would have inflicted some pain on the girl.

Amelio yelled out to let him go, he was okay he wasn't going to hit her back, Michael let Amelio go…. Amelio straightened himself out, Honey I'm not the only sinner your husband was just as bad and I could prove it. I didn't kill your husband he was not all that for me to go crazy over. Plus its not in my nature to kill a person I only show them love. Amelio became that dangerous person Michael spoke about…. I will tell you one thing I did fuck you husband…. I fucked him hard Amelio began to tease the girl I fucked the shit out of his long meaty AMELIO I stopped him…. Hmm I could still taste it in my mouth. Michael made a gagging noise and we all looked at him he waved his hands indicating that he was fine then moved away for a bit.

The girl lunged at Amelio to hit him again, this time I got in her way with my fist ready. I said if you put your hands on my brother one more time I am going to drag your ass up and down this fucking sidewalk. Amelio shot back at the young girl he said Nancy look. The girl looked surprised at the fact that Amelio knew her name. Amelio continued listen if I would've known that Kevin was married to you I would not have given into his flirting. Nancy said he was not flirting with you, you bastard you forced him to do those things, he told me everything! Amelio looked at Nancy and with a soft tone he said… I never forced Kevin to do anything he didn't want to do, he was the one that wanted it to happen. I didn't even know he was married until you answered his cell phone that day a few weeks ago. Nancy he didn't wear a wedding ring in the office, that led me to believe that he wasn't married. Nancy had tears in her eyes, the tears now rolling down her cheeks she looked at the both of us.

Nancy said I can't believe this asshole even in death he has played me like a piano. Amelio was being nice after the bitch punched him. Nancy asked is there some where private we can talk? Yeah just not alone my sister and her boyfriend is coming along. Michael and I looked at each other when Amelio made the comment, Michael pulled me closer to him. He whispered in my ear, that has a nice ring to it. Amelio kept talking to Nancy. I looked at Michael and batted my eyes. Amelio looked at both of us with an evil stare. Michael and I stopped giggling and continued to pay attention to Amelio and Nancy. We missed a whole portion of their conversation. Next thing Michael and I were watching Amelio open the car door for Nancy, then had the nerves to say well lets go somewhere private to talk, she has something to tell me. Michael and I got into the car, Amelio said no what are you doing stay out there. Michael looked at Amelio like he was crazy. Michael said how about I drop you two off at the Restaurant Bar and Grille its noisy all the time and you two will have your privacy. Amelio nodded his head at Michael.

Michael looked in my direction and shrugged his shoulders, we both hoped in the car. Nancy was sitting in the back seat crying, Amelio being as nice as is was comforting her. I thought to myself, what does this girl have up her sleeves. Once we were all inside of the car Michael turned on the ignition and drove a few blocks to get to the Restaurant Bar and Grille in the West End.

Chapter Ten

Once we arrived at the bar and grille, and Michael and I were ready to take off. Amelio said no come inside with us please…. We all walked inside of the restaurant, the setting was the same from when I was here with Dylan a few weeks back. Michael and I walked up to the bar and waved the bartender down. When we had his attention Michael took charge, he asked for a private booth in which no one will bother us. The bartender looked at Michael and pointed to the back of the room, the bartender said that's as private as it's going to get. Nancy looked around, I don't want everyone to hear what I have to say to you. I looked at Nancy and said if it was that important it shouldn't matter where you say it. Nancy looked at Amelio then at me…. Does she really have to be here? Amelio answered quickly YES! Nancy nodded her head and followed us to the section the bartender had pointed out to us.

We were all sitting when Michael came out and said I need a drink anybody else wants one. We all told Michael what we wanted, I had asked for a Cola, Amelio said he wanted a shot of cognac and Nancy shocked us all when she asked for a double shot of Tequila….. Amelio broke the silence when he said okay Nancy we are somewhere private, now what is it you need to tell me or better yet what is it you need to talk to me about? Nancy grabbed a napkin from the dispenser that was on the middle of the table, to wipe the tears that gushed down her cheeks. Nancy said I knew Kevin was cheating on me, I just didn't know it was with another man. When we first got together we were freshmen at ROC Community College, we hit it off really quick. He was sensitive, sweet and amazing in bed. We finished our two years at ROC, I had decided to continue going to college so when I had a family we would have something to fall back on. Anyways I started attending ECC College, Kevin and I had separated. I had not heard from Kevin in two years and out of the blue, I get a call from Kevin telling me he got excepted into one of the most respected schools in Massachusetts on a scholarship. Couldn't understand how he had gotten into the school, he wasn't the brightest person, he always got by on his looks and his charm. Amelio said I could vouch for that.

Nancy continued well we kept in contact and we would go out from time to time, the follow fall he had called me and said his plan was falling into place all he needed was a wife at his side supporting him every step of the way. Nancy looked at me, she had the same facial expression on her face I had when Joshua had left me. It was a sad puppy look…. The look that said what will happen to me next? How will I handle everything and take care of myself when I always had someone there to help me look….

Nancy continued telling us how happy she was they had gotten married right after she was finished with school. I don't know how I could've been so stupid, Kevin kept taking courses and internships moving from one law firm to the next. Then at one particular law firm he had a sexual harassment complaint, he won the case against the lawyer. A few months after she had lost the case she committed suicide. At first I was sick to my stomach, but when Kevin came home a few weeks ago in the morning and said he had gone out drinking with you, and when I noticed the hickey on his back I did question him about it. Kevin told me you've been stalking him and on that night you had gotten him drink…. Nancy had drank the tequila in one swoosh, ah that was good! Michael had asked if she wanted another one and Nancy replied yes. Wiping her tears again with the napkin she had taken from the dispenser.

Nancy continued with her story…. That night Kevin came into our bedroom with tears in his eyes he told me you made him do awful things against his will and that you threatened him that if he wants to be a lawyer he needed to do as you told him too…. Michael came back with the drinks, Michael said Nancy that's your name right? Nancy nodded her head, I don't mean to butt in, just look at Amelio if I didn't want him to do something or force me to do something I didn't want to do I would easily toss him to the side especially if we were both drunk. Nancy said I'm just telling him what Kevin told me about Amelio when he was at home that night. I grabbed Michael's leg insinuating to stay quiet, after he jerked a bit he nodded his head in agreement. Amelio came out from his silence, well everything he had told you about me was a lie except for the two of us sleeping together. Not only can I prove that I didn't force anything upon Kevin, I can show you and again if I knew that Kevin was married I would've never dealt with him…. Nancy wiped the tears from her face for the umpteenth time…. So Amelio you have proof? Amelio nodded his head, Yup I sure do.

Carmella, Amelio said my name give me the camcorder! Amelio I left it in the house I'm sorry was I suppose to bring it with me? I couldn't stand to see this girl suffering anymore the suspicion I had earlier was gone all I felt for Nancy was sorry that she is going through all this, I couldn't even console her she was a stranger to me… yet we were close in what we have gone through with the men we love so much.

Amelio glared at me, Carmella give me the fucking camcorder! I couldn't stop him this was his business not mine. Michael said baby give it to him…. I reached into my purse that resembled a miniature laundry bag and pulled out the camcorder. Nancy looked surprised, what I was on a hidden camera the whole time? Amelio said no but Kevin was, see I like to watch what I do. I tried to stop I felt bad that Amelio was about to show this young girl what her husband was doing with another man. I gave Amelio the camcorder, Amelio grabbed it more like snatched it out of my hands opened up the camcorder then pressed play, Michael got up quickly from his seat and took large strides to the bar. Amelio turned on the camcorder over to Nancy to show her, he didn't force Kevin to do anything he didn't want to do on his own. At one point I could hear

Amelio asking Kevin if he liked the way it felt. Nancy began to cry uncontrollably. From what I could hear Kevin was moaning and in other parts of the audio was muffled.

I couldn't stand to see this girl suffer anymore I told Amelio to turn off the camcorder I think she got the point. Amelio gave me look that told me to mind my own business, I said in a stronger tone and in Spanish to turn off the camcorder. Amelio knew that I was angry with him at that moment, sorry Nancy I've worked to hard to get where I'm in life and my profession to let someone like Kevin take it all away from me. Michael had came back with the whole bottle of tequila and four shot glasses. Michael said right now I think we all need a drink, I didn't think I would have to hear and witness all if this today it's too much for me to handle in one day. Nancy looked at Michael and said I would need the whole bottle, my life is in the worse place I would think it would ever be, and I don't know how to get out of it…. It's like a bad dream.

Michael poured out the first shot of tequila and handed it to Nancy…. Here drink this it'll make you feel better. Nancy grabbed the shot glass while Michael poured the other shot glasses for the rest of us. Nancy had finished hers and was asking for more. She said I can't believe he has done this to me, I'm sorry we put you through so much I believe that bastard with all the lies he had told me. He said he had a case against you for sexual harassment I'm going to tell them to drop it. I still don't understand why he was in your apartment dead. Amelio said he knew where my spare key was I had told him the many times we had spoken to each other. I was in Puerto Rico when it happened…. The police have all my video tapes from my security cameras so I am really going at it blind. Michael had poured Nancy another shot of Tequila. Nancy said I can't believe I was married to a con artist, Amelio said where was Kevin before he started his internship with us at Dave and Barley. Nancy said I don't know the name of the law firm, what I do know is that he was always driving back and forth to Rhode Island, he 1told me the law firm was based there, right next to the court house, why do you ask? Amelio said because I have to prove my innocence before September 1st or I will go to jail for a crime I didn't commit.

Nancy said with tears running down her cheeks again, I can't believe Kevin has put me through so much I just can't believe it. I hope his soul rots in hell for all the pain and damage he has caused everyone including you Amelio. Michael asked what did he do? Nancy looked at Michael with the same facial expression I had on my face. Michael was not on the same page as the rest of us. Nancy answered his question, he has lied to get what he wanted, he fucked the next person over to get to the top without caring what the outcome will be. Now I look the idiot that I let him walk all over me. I believed everything he told me, I was truly blinded by my love for him. Nancy continued whenever I would bring up having a baby and he would say he was not ready. A few weeks ago we found out we were having a baby and Kevin forced me to get rid of the baby.…. He wanted me to have an abortion. Amelio said oh goodness he really was a pro at being a con, he told my boss that I stalked you blaming me for his wife having a miscarriage. Kevin had said word for word "my wife was so stressed from Amelio constantly calling that it caused my wife to lose the child she was carrying. It was suppose to be our first born child." my boss said he had tears rolling down his face and all. Now I know it was an act.

Amelio begged Nancy to testify on his behalf, he would get her a notebook so she could write down everything she has told him. Amelio said I need this to get my reputation back into good standings, if not I would lose my license to practice law like the other lawyer Kevin fucked over. Nancy nodded her head, she grabbed the bottle of Tequila poured herself another drink. Nancy was beginning to feel tipsy, she was no longer crying she was angry. Nancy said fuck how could I be so stupid hitting her forehead with the palm of her hand. Nancy was past tipsy she looked at Amelio and said your nice for a gay guy. When I punched you in the face you didn't hit me back, Amelio said yeah I think the Tequila is starting to get to you. Why don't you have something to eat? Nancy had downed two shots of Tequila back to back. I looked at Michael and asked why did you get the whole bottle? Michael responded by shrugging his shoulders I don't know I thought it was the right thing to do at that the time… with Amelio showing him the video of his love affair with her husband. Nancy was beginning to talk non sense. Michael said Nancy I'm going to take the bottle back to the bar. Nancy was not paying attention to what Michael had said. Nancy said you know how a woman can tell when she is ready to tell when she is ready to leave her husband, you know how Amelio's sister? I said no I don't! Nancy said well when you start thinking about was to do your husband in. I was shocked at what Nancy had jut said…. What did you just say? Repeating herself she said when you think of ways to do him in.

I thought about putting ammonia in his drinks, my sister is the owns a cleaning company, she said ammonia hydroxide works. I said Nancy you need to stop as she kept throwing out ideas on how to kill her deceased husband. Amelio and I looked at each other, listened to the way she was talking. Amelio was soaking it up. He was using the Tequila to his advantage. Michael was absolutely right about Amelio he is a dangerous man when he is angry. I leaned closer to Michael I whispered in his ears lets get this girl home before Amelio takes full advantage of her. Michael nodded his head, then said good idea. Nancy said where do you order the food? I could go for fried chicken and potato skins…. Amelio said hmm that sounds good, Michael could you be a doll and order some food for us. I answered for Michael, I said Amelio it's time to go, Amelio gave me the evil look again…. He said sis I'm hungry and so is Nancy, how about we order some food and then we leave.

I said okay Amelio after we eat the food we are leaving, Michael had the day off and he wants to go spend some time with his sister. Amelio gave me a stupid look he asked in Spanish his sister or his other girlfriend? I looked at Michael and gave him a fake smile, then I looked back at Amelio don't start. Amelio please she's tipsy and you know it, don't be an asshole. Amelio put on his drama queen act by telling everyone how he spent the week end in prison, and that all he wanted was something good to eat. Carmella it's okay I will get them something to munch o, Michael was being very patient with us, then he looked at Amelio and said after you eat I'm taking everyone to where they belong and I'm going to pick up my sister. Amelio smiled at Michael and asked how old is your sister? Michael said twenty two… I knew what Amelio was up to and I didn't like it. Michael as soon as everyone eats we need to take this girl home, or at least call someone to pick her up. Nancy began to slur her words I am just fine the I's sounding longer than usual…. All I need is some food to eat and my beautiful sister will come and pick me up, Michael you would like her. Amelio jumped in and said Nancy I told you Michael is my sister's boyfriend did you forget? I said it when we got in the car. Nancy was giggling as she looked at Michael in a flirting way. Nancy asked Michael, hey Michael have you ever had white pussy before? it's like eating chicken, fondling herself trying to seduce Michael.

Michael and I looked at each other he was the bold one to say no I don't believe I have, I did have some Spanish beaver dam that taste like Caramel nice and sweet…. I couldn't help but to laugh at what Michael had said. Of course Amelio being a prune said EWWW that is nasty and I don't need to hear that before I eat my food. I said oh please Amelio it's okay not everyone can please you…. Now what do you want to eat? I have things to do and people to see…. Amelio said I haven't seen you in a few weeks your clients can wait one more day. Amelio was acting spoiled I said in a strong tone of voice, no they can't especially when I used what I had in my savings on you. I have to make it all back up…. Amelio said don't worry once I am cleared of all the charges the money used on the bail is given back to the person that paid it.

Amelio and I were deep into our dialogue when Nancy said out of the blue I will help you with whatever you need Amelio. Amelio looked at me with the see I told you so look! Nancy I would greatly appreciate it, now enough talk let's get something to eat. Nancy grabbed the bottle of Tequila, and poured herself another drink. Nancy you don't know me from a hole in a wall, yet I'm going to give you some advice…. Drinking will not solve your problems all it will do is suppress the pain you feel for that moment. When you wake the next day all those awful memories will hit you at once leaving you in a depression that you won't know what to do with yourself, I know because I've been there. I wrote my number on a napkin… here in case you need someone to talk to you can call me…. Amelio looked at me, he asked what about me? When I needed someone to talk to you were never there for me. You were too busy spending time with Michael and I had to depend on Mom to listen to my problems. Nancy grabbed the napkin and put it inside of her purse, she also grabbed the bottle of Tequila and poured herself yet another shot, this time she took it down like a professional…. After putting the shot glass down Nancy went into her purse again and pulled out her cellphone. She dialed one number on her phone then brought the phone up to her ear.

Nancy said hey Maggie can you pick me up? All you can hear was Nancy slurring her words… well I'll talk to you later. The phone call lasted about two minutes before she hung up the phone. I asked Nancy, is your sister picking you up? She shook her head from side to side no, she said I guess you have to take the train home. Michael said where is home? Nancy looked at all of us and said Weymouth. Michael and I looked at each other, we can't let you get on the train like this, you can crash at my place until you sober up. Nancy nodded her head, then thanked us for being so nice to her after what she had did. I was trying not to look at Amelio I could feel him grilling me and shaking that one leg when he's angry. Amelia came out and said what the fuck do you think your doing? I ignored Amelio. The food had arrived, and Amelio sat there quietly I couldn't read him, he was someone else I did not know who my brother was turning into, and I didn't like it. When it was time to leave I thanked Michael for everything he had done for me that day, I also apologized for all the craziness that he had to endure. I had to admit other than my other customers this was an adventure for me.

Michael kissed me on the forehead then said it was alright, as he helped Nancy back to the car so she wouldn't stumble all over and fall. I turned to walk to the car with Michael when I was stopped by Amelio, Carmella what the hell are you doing? Did you forget who she is? No but I do know you forgot who you were, and how Mom raised us. Amelio said no I did not forget that bitch and her husband set me up to ruin my life how do you expect me to act? Nice because her husband is dead oh fucking well he deserved it for being a complete asshole and wanting to fuck people over just to make a few quick bucks. Amelio you are going through some shit I understand that, it still does not give you the right to treat people like shit. Please stop acting like a spoiled bitch and get in the car. Amelio rolled his eyes at me then got inside of the car without saying another word.

Once we were all inside of the car I told Michael to take me home first since I was closer to the bar, and I didn't think Nancy would make it in his car if he dropped Amelio off first. Carmella you're right he opened up the windows to give Nancy some fresh air. Michael had not turned on the ignition when he was trying to speed out of the parking lot. I put my hand on Michael's lap and looked out of the window at the side mirror, the way it was positioned I could see a portion of Amelio's face, he was pouting the whole ride to my complex which did not take long at all. He brought everything upon himself for not thinking before acting now he has to deal with it. Michael came up to the building within minutes, I got out of the car and helped Nancy to the doors, when I entered the double doors I noticed Jerry had returned to work. Hey little miss you need some help there? Knowing what he had just recently gone through I replied… no thank you she's just having a rough day…. And before I forget welcome back! This time take it easy, Jerry nodded his head as he said no problem. I got Nancy to the elevator, she looked around and said this is a nice building, I live in a low income apartment and it's nothing compared to this. I knew she was drunk all I could say was thank you then I pressed for my level and headed upstairs.

when we got to the front of my door Nancy said she wasn't feeling well, I pulled out the keys and opened the door to my apartment to let her in. Nancy walked inside and gave her head a twirl almost as a quick glance around the apartment, she found the living and stumbled to the couch then plopped down on it. I ran into the kitchen to grab the pail I use to pour the cleaning liquid, so it was smelling fresh, I made my way to the living room as fast as I could I didn't want this bitch ruining my rug with the smell of vomit. When I got to Nancy she said I know your brother is a lawyer…. What the hell do you do for a living? Well my brother is a lawyer your right and I am an escort, I wasn't going to lie to the woman by the time she sobered up she would've forgotten what I had just told her. Nancy asked isn't that illegal. I nodded my head then said only if you don't have the right papers to make it a legal business in which I do. Nancy told me how my apartment was nice before she let go of the food and alcohol from her system and into the pail. I helped her by pulling her hair back to make it easier for her. Nancy lifted her head…. I feel better she told me as she laid back on the couch for a couple of minutes before she leaned forward again to repeat the same action in letting her food out into the pail for the second time. I should be fine now all I need is some sleep to sober up and I will leave.

I said don't worry you have been through a lot with my brother and your husband just relax get some sleep and when you are refreshed you can leave. Nancy nodded her head in agreement with what I had said. I left her side for a moment to get a pillow and blanket out of the closet, the ones I give to Amelio when he crashes here…. How ironic. When I got back to the living room I found that Nancy was already sleeping. I covered her with the blanket I was feeling tired myself after putting up with so much I walked into my bedroom placed the phone on my night stand and threw myself onto the bed closing my eyes not remembering when I fell asleep…. I woke up to the sound of cell phone vibrating on the night stand thinking it was someone who needed my services I hit the silent button and sent it into voice mail… a few seconds later the house phone began to ring I knew it could have only been Amelio or my mother. I answered the phone…. Hello in a groggy voice. Carmella were you sleeping? Amelio was on the other line. I said no not anymore what's going on? Is that bitch still in your apartment if she is you better make sure she didn't steal anything while you were sleeping. I know she is up to something I could feel it.

I told Amelio I was too tired to deal with any of his shit and the reason she was there was his fault…. Amelio you got her too drunk to ride the train because you wanted to she what would come out if you were to give her all this alcohol, and it worked you should be ashamed of yourself. Amelio played it off like he didn't know what I was talking about. Don't act like I'm stupid I caught on to your game along time ago and to be honest with you I don't know who you're becoming. I can tell you this I don't like it Amelio and you need to stop it now! Amelio became the drama queen once more you Carmella ever since you and Michael hooked up you have changed and remember the last time you were with Joshua I was there to pick up the pieces, don't expect me to be there for you this time around. I was hurt by what Amelio had said so I cut the phone call short. I told Amelio you're a real bitch, I have to go check on this girl call me when you're ready to apologize to me and you are welcomed for bailing you out today. I didn't give Amelio the chance to respond to what I had told him I hung up the phone. I got out of the bed and walked into the living room to see Nancy still sleeping on the couch. I thought to myself what am I going to do now.... I would have to wait until tomorrow to start answering all the missed calls I had from my clients. I was going to call Michael instead I hopped back into my bed and went back to sleep thinking tomorrow was a new day.

Chapter Eleven

I woke up the next day forgetting that I had someone sleeping on my couch when I walked into the living room I could see a head full of dark curls sitting on my couch…. I thought to myself OH SHIT! I had forgotten about this girl…. I walked closer to see that the television was not on and she was just sitting on the couch without moving. I hope this girl did not off herself in my apartment I was starting to like it more. Nancy are you okay, I didn't hear you wake up I thought that you would at least tell me you were leaving. I kept talking as I inched myself closer to the couch. When I finally reached the couch I gave Nancy a nudge to get her out of her trance. Nancy looked at me with tears in her eyes, why did this happen to me? I had it all planned out on how I was going to live my life and how I was going to have everything I wanted because I worked hard for it, and now look at me I'm sitting in a strangers apartment with tears in my eyes, my husband had sex with another man and now he is dead how is that possible to happen all in one month.

Nancy I don't know what to tell you, you're sober now and more coherent to what I tell you. Better than last night… I understand you're upset I've had bad relationships in which I was dumped for the model of the week…. I couldn't let that be the end of me, I needed and I wanted more so I got into the escort service business. I run my own life if the person is gay bi sexual or tri sexual it won't bother me anymore because I learned to only worry about myself….

Nancy looked at me with the WHAT THE FUCK ARE YOU TALKING ABOUT LOOK! The point I am trying to make is this I will always do what I want without anyone stopping me, yeah you lost your husband who wasn't really thinking about you he just wanted someone to take care of him. He did what he had to do so why can't you do the same. Get your shit together bury the mother fucker that fucked you over and call it a day.... It sounds harsh but think about it. I sat next to Nancy and rubbed her back, without hesitation Nancy turned her face closer moving closer to me and kissed me passionately. I had never been with another woman before yet it felt good.

Nancy was aggressive, the moisture and softness of her lips pressed up against mine made me wet. I returned the kiss to see how far it would go.... Nancy realizing what she was doing pulled away, I enjoyed the kiss and wanted more. Nancy brought her hands up to her lips as tears formed in her eyes.... Sorry I don't know what I was thinking, I just wanted to see what Kevin felt when he was with another man. At that time I wasn't thinking about Kevin or Amelio I wanted to finish what Nancy had started inside of me. We were like virgins when it came to being with another woman. I moved closer to Nancy putting my hands on her head I said it's okay I enjoyed it.

I have never been with another woman except for a hermaphodite but that doesn't count. Did you enjoy the kiss? Nancy nodded her head yes I actually did is that a sin? I didn't know how to answer.... I moved her head closer and this time I kissed her with a soft passionate kiss.... Are you comfortable? I moved my hand to feel her soft squeezable breast that she hid behind the throw pillow she clutched in her hands. I moved the pillow to see how I groped her breast. I moved closer almost on top of Nancy and felt her up some more. My kisses moved from Nancy's lips down to her neck slowly making my way down to her breast as I unbuttoned her blouse with one hand. Only to reveal the D- cup that nicely complimented her breast.

I moved my hand back to her breast when I was done undoing her blouse, squeezing them together I brought my tongue down to the middle of her cleavage sucking just on the top. I looked up without moving away to see Nancy's facial expression. Nancy had he head leaned tilted back in pleasure. I continued to move my tongue in circular motion until I reached the base of her nipple, and sucking on it with delight. I could hear Nancy whispering I want more! I moved away from Nancy and told her to take off her pants…. Nancy did as she was told she stood up, took off her pants and underwear revealing a nicely shaved area. I grabbed her hand and laid her back on the couch, spreading her legs apart and went in without thinking my tongue played with her clitoris. I moved my tongue in circular motion sucking on the skin that laid there. I was enjoying the taste that flowed out of Nancy.

I felt her body convulse as she climaxed in mouth and all over my face, the sweetness that poured into my mouth was tasty… I took my pointer finger and squeezed it into her vagina feeling the wetness that came out of her. I stood up to see Nancy's facial expression she still wanted more. I was my turn to feel what she had felt, I stripped off the night gown I was wearing exposing my body. Nancy sat up on the couch, grabbed my hips and brought me closer to her face. I could feel as she used the tip of her tongue to play with the flat stomach that stood in front of her. I grabbed the massive curls with one hand lifted my leg onto the couch and felt as Nancy went in without thinking twice. She knew exactly where to place her tongue and how to move it. My legs beginning to shake from the excitement that was building up inside of me. Moved Nancys head and went from standing to laying on the couch. I spread my legs to show the arrow that pointed down to my spot. Nancy took two of her fingers and stuck them inside of me almost reaching my G Spot. I couldn't believe the feeling that was taking over my body, not even Michael made me feel his sensation. Nancy fingered me, she went in and out a few times then brought her tongue down to finish off what her fingers had started.

My body moved from side to side as I enjoyed every movement Nancy made with her tongue. The way she swiveled her tongue round and round made my body go crazy, at that moment I knew I had to have more female clients, especially if they made me feel this way. I closed my eyes as Nancy worked her magic…. Aw I could hear myself as she brought me to my climax. I grabbed the full head of curls and shoved her face deeper into my inner thighs as I let out all that would come out of me. When Nancy lifted her head we both giggled, I guess you got over Kevin, Nancy stopped giggling if I knew what Kevin was doing in the first place instead of being so naïve I would have done this a long time ago…. I feel sorry for your brother he was hurt and murdering someone is not a way to get over it. If your brother would have came to me with the video I would have killed Kevin myself and then pleaded insanity and we would have all gone on with our lives. Now I can't help him much but to tell what Kevin had told me.

I couldn't listen to it right now I had good sex and I was hungry, I changed the subject…. Nancy are you hungry because I am starving I need to get the energy back that you took from me. Nancy nodded her head we both got up off the couch to put on our clothes, the buzzer to the apartment began to ring. I walked over to the intercom as Nancy continued to get dressed. Hello…. I let go of the intercom to see who was ringing my bell. Hey it's Michael I brought some breakfast. I thought to myself perfect timing, I pressed the button to let him into the complex. I ran to the bathroom to get the air freshener that I kept under the sink. I sprayed the whole house, I wanted the smell of sex to vanish fast. I surely didn't want Michael to know what I just did. Once I was done with the air freshener I ran to put it back where I had gotten it from inside of the bathroom. I walked back into the living room to find Michael at the door staring at me…. I see that you still have company. Yeah we were having a girl talk. You came at the perfect time we were telling each other how hungry we were, and boom you showed up with breakfast you are an angel….. Michael gave me an interesting look, sure anything for my baby…. Michael stood at the door still, hey honey can I talk to you in the bedroom. Michael gave Nancy the food he had in his hand and walked with me towards the bedroom. When we got inside of the bedroom Michael began to whisper so that Nancy won't hear him speak….. He said what are you doing? I've already told you about having strangers in your apartment. Please doing that shit,

Michael continued to talk as my mind wondered to the time ahead where Nancy and I had just a few moments ago. Carmella are you listening to me, I'm trying to help you out here. Snapping out of my trance with a smile on my face, yes baby I'm listening to you… I remember what you said to me before and believe me she is innocent. Michael gave me a funny look as I said come on let's go eat, it's too early in the morning to be a sour pus, besides I called you last night and you didn't answer the phone.

Michael looked at me with the puppy dog look on his face, I love that look that's why I didn't tell him about me and Nancy. Hey honey I'm sorry I got the call his morning after taking your brother home I went home and straight to bed. All the drama you two have is unbelievable. I listened to Michael he was right I snapped back, I said you're right Michael and that's why I stick to myself. Oh and I see what you meant when you said Amelio is a dangerous man when he is angry, and when he wants something really bad. Michael you got that on point and you have only known him for a short period of time. Michael said yeah I'm good at reading peoples personalities and your brother is obvious. I looked away and quickly changed the subject, okay let's go eat I'm starving… Michael put his arm around my waist and kissed me gently on the lips, he quickly moved away and asked did you have a client last night or this morning? I shook my head NO…. are you sure? Yes Michael I am sure Michael what's up? Nothing Michael shrugged his shoulders….. Nothing never mind. If he didn't ask again I was going to put more emphasis on the subject. We walked out of the room and into the kitchen where Nancy was sitting already helping herself to some breakfast.

She looked at Michael I have to get going so I can catch the Ten o'clock commuter train. Michael asked which way are you going again? I can see if I could drop you off…. I'm going south to Weymouth. Well Michael said I have to go to Dedham if you want the ride I can take you to Braintree that's the closest I can get you. We have to leave now. I knew Michael was trying to get Nancy out of my apartment. Nancy looked at me then at Michael. I'll stay and have breakfast with Carmella, I could catch the next train out to Weymouth. I can even go on shopping, I haven't seen the inside of a department store in a long time. Michael said in a concerned tone are you sure I can give you the ride. Nancy looked at Michael again…. Don't worry I'll be fine…. Michael said okay then you girls behave yourself, don't go crazy on your shopping spree and end up in debt. Nancy and I said we won't at the same time like two school girls and then giggled. Michael gave me a look as to be careful then said I will leave you two ladies I have to go to work. I said we will after were done eating, Michael gave me another quick peck on the cheeks and left out of the door.

After I ran to the door to lock it I told Nancy I was going to take a shower and eat when I got out. When I'm done I'll give you some clothes to wear you look like you fit some of my old clothes from when I was with Joshua. I walked over to the bathroom to wash up, I turned the water on and began to take off my clothes I was ready to take the smell of vagina juice off of me. Michael had smelt it when he was here I know he did. Before I could get inside of the shower Nancy was behind me ready to go for another round. I could see that she wasn't going to take no for an answer. Nancy got as close as she could rubbing her body against mine. She whispered in my ear, I want you in the shower…. I couldn't help it I wanted her too. The feeling of another woman touching and feeling up on me excited me. I stood naked in the bathroom as Nancy rubbed me down with her soft hands. I wanted her just as much as she wanted me. I helped Nancy rip off her clothes so I could feel her smooth Vanilla skin one more time.

We both got into the shower letting the water drip down on our bodies as we kissed passionately. I thought to myself what was I doing this is the wife of the man found dead in my brothers house, and here I am having passionate sex with this woman we hugged and cuddled as we got out of the shower, and straight to the bed. I helped Nancy lie down slowly kissing and nibbling on her skin. I made my way down her flat onto her belly button and down into her inner thighs. I could feel the wetness of her vagina, using the middle and index finger I thrust them into Nancy using the tip of my tongue I tickled Nancy's clitoris. In the back of my mind I thought about

Michael is this considered cheating we're not committed to each other… were just dating.

Hey it's my turn Nancy's voice piercing through my thoughts of Michael. I felt her fingers running through my curls lifting up my head. I stood up and crawled onto the bed staying on my hands and knees I felt as Nancy shoved her fingers into my vagina…. I could feel her fingers thrusting in and out of me faster and faster. I finally climaxed for the final time, Nancy got up and walked into the bathroom and turned on the shower. I walked into the closet still naked and pulled out the trunk of old clothes, I had something in there that would fit Nancy…. I thought back when I was with Joshua I was very thin because Joshua wanted his woman to be fit and thin. After I broke up with Joshua and the fact that I was doing well all by myself, I gained more weight so I know that the clothes I have now won't fit Nancy. I looked through the clothes and found a few pictures of me and Joshua smiling….. I ripped those up why should I hold on to old memories when they were bad. I could make new ones.

Nancy came out of the bathroom bare naked the water still dripping off her body…. Hey Carmella do you have a towel I can use? I grabbed the towel I had in the closet and tossed it to Nancy along with a pair of tights and a tank top, then walked back into the closet to get some comfortable clothes for myself. I walked past Nancy I thought to myself was this like having sex with Stan the client with the extra genital part….. Am I like Amelio now do I need to join the gay community now, and not only that Nancy had a lot of experience with what she was doing….. Oh no did she play me was Michael right about letting people into my apartment without knowing them, they could rob me or even worse kill me. My mind was gong crazy I didn't know what to else to think. I quickly turned off the shower got dressed and left out of the bathroom, when walked into the room Nancy wasn't in there anymore. Where the hell is she my apartment is not that big so I know she didn't go too far….

I walked out into the living room to see if she was in there and sure enough she was stilling at the bar smiling and laughing quietly on her cell phone…. These people are just like you said honey real stupid…. They fell for the my husband is dead woe is me. The last words I heard were yeah I'm still in her apartment and found the safe it was that easy, well we're about to leave so you can do your thing call me when your done…. I walked into the room before Nancy could noticed that I was there. When Nancy came back into the room she played it off like nothing happened…. Hey you ready to go shopping? I couldn't contain myself the anger built up real fast, are you fucking kidding me I just heard your whole little talk with who ever you were on the phone with and I think you better leave now, I walked over to the house phone…. I'm calling the police on your ass trying to play me for a sucker! Bitch you must be out your got damn mind, yeah I caught on to your game. Once I picked up the phone Nancy was quick on her feet so she knew exactly what she was doing.

I felt a strong blow to my face the house phone fell out of my hand and onto the floor. I had dialed 911 before she could get to me. I quickly got back up and began to struggle with Nancy, for a skinny bitch she had some strength to her. Next thing I know I pushed her with all I had inside of me. Nancy went back and just laid on the floor without moving, I got closer and gave her a nudge with my foot yet no response…. I could hear a females voice in the distance I looked to see if I could find the house phone. I picked it up to hear the woman's voice come through loud and clear…. Hello is anybody there if so please answer the phone, the police will be at your door in a few minutes. Still a bit disoriented from the punch Nancy had given me…. I said hello I'm here please send me and ambulance she's no moving. Just before I could hang up the phone there was a knock at the door. I ran to the door and opened it…. In the door way stood the two police officers the dispatcher had spoken about.

The officers asked is everything alright? I said no she is in the room we had a fight and now she's not moving…. One of the officers walked past me and into the room while the other stood by my side and comforted me. Letting me know the ambulance was on the way…. When the police offer walked out of the room e had a serious expression as he used his radio, I barely made out what he was saying. He walked up to me then said miss you need to turn around and place your hands behind your back. I did as I was told, I could feel the officer hand cuffing me. When I turned around after being hand cuffed the officer began to read my Mirada rights, when Michael had walked into the apartment…. What's going on where is she? He ran into the bedroom the officer went in after him. Michael came out with his hands over his face, no it wasn't suppose to happen…. The officer took Michael to one corner and asked him a few questions…. The smaller thinner officer asked me how did I know him? I told him we have been dating for a few weeks now. The tall officer called his partner over to him and whispered something into his ear.

They both walked over to me and said Ms. Ortega you are under arrest for the murder of Nancy Spritzer…. I said what how is that possible? Michael tell them who she is…. Michael said I just did, you just murdered my fiance. My mind went blank I couldn't think straight I put two and two together he was the person on the other line of Nancy's cell phone…. You mother fucker all this time you were plotting against me I can't believe this shit. I got something for your ass, watch your back. The officers said miss you can't make threats now let's go…. All the neighbors were out their apartments watching as the officers escorted me out of my apartment.

I thought to myself wow fucked over by a man again… four weeks later I was convicted of murder and soliciting. Now I am here telling you my story and the worse part of it all is that I just found out I am pregnant and Michael is out there conning someone else. Matilda looked surprised…. Baby girl don't worry we will take good care of you and that baby in here. And as for Michael he will get what he deserves…. I closed my eyes yeah he will get what he deserves, I will make sure of it.